LETTERS
—FROM—
BRAZIL
III

Good Times to Sad Times

MARK J. CURRAN

Order this book online at www.trafford.com
or email orders@trafford.com

Most Trafford titles are also available at major online book retailers.

"Letters from Brazil III" is in English, however, many Brazilian Portuguese terms and short
dialogues are maintained for their flavor, but translated as well into English."

Print information available on the last page.

ISBN: 978-1-4907-9896-7 (sc)
ISBN: 978-1-4907-9897-4 (e)

Trafford rev. 01/02/2020

 www.trafford.com

North America & international
toll-free: 1 888 232 4444 (USA & Canada)
fax: 812 355 4082

1

PERSONAL PLANS ASUNDER

I'm Mike Gaherty a professor at the University of Nebraska in Lincoln. I returned from a scary time in Brazil last September in 1970 and taught the past academic year in Lincoln. The reader might recall that I had plans to marry long-time college sweetheart Molly from Georgetown and D.C. days, in fact we had the date set for June of this year 1971. With her in faraway Washington D.C. and me out here in the boonies in Lincoln, we tried to keep the wedding plans and romance going with long phone calls and an occasional visit. I think the "monkey wrench" in the whole affair was when I told Molly just a few weeks ago in the late winter of 1971 that I would have to go back to Brazil this next summer for a whole lot of reasons. My promised book in Pernambuco was still not out and that hinge had to be oiled! I was told in no uncertain terms by the Modern Languages chairman at the University of Nebraska that if I wanted to keep my job, it was "publish or perish" and there's a big difference between my promises to him (all in good faith) and publications laid on the table in front of the tenure committee!

And there was the situation and opportunity to be much more with famous Brazilian Popular Music's Chico Buarque de Hollanda in the summer of 1971 and do joint projects on "Cordel" and his music, projects that potentially would have incredible visibility in Brazil and would be a "gold mine" for me in the academic milieu in the U.S.

I pleaded with Molly to postpone the wedding until semester break of the following academic year, December of 1971 or January of 1972, that all that was happening was a real emergency for me at the U. of Nebraska. But what might have topped all this off was when I admitted to Molly that I would be seeing one-time Brazilian girlfriend Cristina Maria again, out of necessity, because it was she who had set up the entire Chico Buarque possibility. Molly, no stranger to my romantic past with Cristina Maria, blew her stack at that point. "I thought you said you would not be going to Brazil in 1971, that you could do all your research here, and that we would get married as planned and settle down in Lincoln. Now I hear this 'hot' Brazilian chick is back on the scene! Jesus, Gaherty, what kind of a fool do you think I am? You promised fidelity before we were engaged and that was a farce and didn't exactly happen, so now it's even worse. I can't understand how your damned job and me can't both work out. Forget our agreement; I'll keep that cheap Brazilian engagement ring as a souvenir. I've got lots of other possibilities. Goodbye." She slammed down the receiver and I was sitting stunned at the end of the line. Christ! She didn't even give me a chance to repeat that Cristina Maria was engaged herself, had told me she could never live in the U.S. and knowing I couldn't live or move to Brazil. "Merda!" Romance or sex with that Brazilian woman was not even on my mind. It was research, keeping my job and getting tenure that was a priority.

So, was it Molly's knee-jerk reaction or my impatience and lack of "diplomacy" to work it all out? I don't know. I'm saying it's not my fault that things turned out a lot different.

2

RESEARCH, CHICO BUARQUE'S
RETURN, THE PHONE CALL

Before I go on with what happened later, I've got to fill in what I was busy with in the 1970-1971 school term with research and updates from Brazil before the marriage plans fell apart. This is important stuff.

Fall 1970 – The Trans-Amazon Project. I mentioned in the epilogue of "Letters II" of 1970 that Brazilian General Garrastazu Médici had a brainstorm with his advisers ["assessores"] after seeing no solution to the droughts and problems in the Northeast; they discovered that the Amazon might serve several good purposes for the regime, first among them the carrying out of the Military's motto of "March to the West" ["Marcha ao Oeste"], Brazil's "Manifest Destiny"! (Notwithstanding the suspicion and nervousness of the Spanish American Amazon neighbors like Colombia, Venezuela, Ecuador, Peru and even Chile, aware of Brazil's alliance with the U.S. and its military and economic aid). The "March" would open up the entire rich Amazon basin to exploration and exploitation of its resources, in 1971 still pretty much of a mystery. There was more – it could be a "safety valve" to that pesky problem of the masses of poor farmers and seasonal workers in the dry Northeast! It would diminish "social pressure" on the periphery of the big cities like Recife. The regime invented a sort of "homesteaders" plan, kind of like the old U.S. "Fifty Acres and a Mule," but with a Brazilian flavor. My research theme and "bread and butter" were the many titles of the "Literatura de Cordel," titles of the highest optimism: "The Transamazonic Carving Through the Forest," ["A Transamazônica Rasgando a Selva"], "Onward and Upward, Transamazonic"

["Pra' Frente, Transamazônica"], "The Poor and the Transamazonic" ["O Povo e a Transamazônica"], and finally, "President Médici and the Transamazonic" ["Presidente Médici e a Transamazônica"]. For now, there was great optimism for most all Brazilians, except perhaps for the Amazon natives and a few budding ecologists.

And there was more, my continued reporting on Chico Buarque de Hollanda's songs of protest and dealings with the on-going military government and dictatorship. I had written of Chico's "Pedro Pedreiro" [Pete the Laborer] and especially of "Apesar de Voce" [In Spite of You] in the last letter of 1970. The latest was Chico and friend Toquinho's song actually written when Chico was still in Italy in self-imposed "exile" with Marieta and the baby in 1969 and 1970, but with consequences when they returned to Brazil in early 1971 – "Samba de Orly." In 1969 Chico, Toquinho and Marieta watched, like millions, the landing of men on the moon, had heard and read of the kidnapping of the U.S. ambassador in Brazil, and the crumbling of the Left in Brazil in small groups. Toquinho decided, in spite of everything, to go back to Brazil and left Chico with the melody which Chico put to words of this great song.

> Samba de Orly
> 1970
> Vai meu irmão, pega esse avião ...
> Go, my friend, catch that airplane
> Mas beija o meu Rio de Janeiro ...
> But give my Rio de Janeiro a kiss ...
> Mas não diga nada, que me viu chorando
> But don't say anything, that you saw me crying
> Se se puder, me manda uma notícia boa.
> And if you can, send me a bit of good news.

What is left out of the allowed lyrics for copyright reasons is that Chico tells friend Toquinho he's right to escape the cold of winter in Italy, to give Rio that kiss before some thief takes Rio away, to not tell of the hardships they both suffered in Italy, and have a good time in 'ole Rio.

After Toquinho's departure, the good news was poet, famous diplomat, Brazilian Modernist Poet, and family friend Vinicius de Morais's encouraging Chico to "Come back to Brazil making noise," that all was now better in Brazil, ideas based on false news from an agent of Chico's Philips Recording Studio and a later to be contested note from Glauber Rocha of "New Cinema" fame. Following Vinicius's advice, Chico thought all would start all over, concert dates, record sales, and "back to normal" in Rio with the family. But instead the former fans and the Left believed he had "caved in" to the dictatorship. At the same time the hunting of leftists, imprisonment and torture took place, the propaganda machine of the Military invented the slogans for a bigger and better Brazil! "Ninguém Segura Este País" ["No One Can Keep This Country Down"], "Brasil, P'ra Frente" ["Onward and Upward Brazil!"], and the more ominous "Brasil – Ame-o o Deixe-O" ["Brazil, Love It or Leave It"].

I wrote all about this still in Lincoln mostly based on library work and news magazines and newspapers from Brazil and sent it as a "Letter" to James Hansen of the "New York Times." During the fall of 1970 in Lincoln after my time in Rio in the summer of 1970 and ongoing in the winter of the spring term of 1971, there were a couple of surprise telephone calls from Chico himself – "Safer than the mail these days." That was what encouraged me to change plans (yikes!) and go back to Rio in the summer of 1971. But something happened that added to all that.

3

AIR MAIL – SPECIAL DELIVERY

In late Spring, 1971, I was still in Lincoln after the blowup with Molly. I was settled down in the apartment and up at the office most days getting ready to continue the research in Brazil when a big surprise came in the mail. Any thoughts of teaching and research were trumped by an air-mail special delivery registered letter from Brazil's Varig Air Line in Los Angeles. I don't get many of those, in fact, this was the first and only. Addressed to Professor Mike Gaherty, University of Nebraska, it said, "We have your international ticket to Rio de Janeiro at the airport and are holding it for you until we hear from you. Depart July 1st, return July 15th." My reaction was, "What in the hell is this?" I called the Varig number (you had to get permission for a long-distance call in the Modern Language Department, tight budgeting!). The Brazilian who answered said, "There's no other information, Mr. Gaherty, but porra! [loosely, "What the f***!"] A free round trip to Rio! You'd be crazy to not take it. You can find something to do for a few days in Rio!" I said I'd call in a day or two to set it up.

They call Brazil the "accidental" country, so this was just one more "accident." That's the way the country runs. I called Varig and made reservations for Los Angeles – Rio and return not knowing what in the world was going on; I did have a wild hunch, academic that is. A good professor always has something in the "drawer," just in case, and I had an academic paper I had written the previous year, thinking of a conference or maybe an article submission in the U.S. I stuffed it into the briefcase along with all the travel documents, packed for a short trip and was soon on my way.

On July 1st I got on an America West flight to L.A. International, enjoyed their complimentary champagne on the way, and walked up to the counter of Varig Airlines after a transfer to the international terminal. When I told the courteous and by the way beautiful and stacked Varig agent (she would appear on the flight as a stewardess) who I was and showed her my letter from Varig, she laughed, asked me if I knew Portuguese, and said, "O senhor ganhou no bicho! ("You just hit the prize" - Brazil's illegal yet legal national lottery). We just received a long telegram from a certain Ana Maria Barbosa from the Casa de Rui Barbosa in Rio explaining the whole thing, including instructions for us to get it to you before the flight. Here it is."

"Miguel, desculpe toda a confusão! ["Pardon all the confusion!"]. We at the Casa de Rui never know from one week, or even one month to the next, about our budget down here, but we hit the jackpot and have full funding for 'O Primeiro Congresso Internacional de Filologia e 'Os Lusíadas' de Luís de Camões.' It all starts July 3rd and will be an amazing meeting. The crème de la crème of the Luso-Brazilian academy, experts in Philology and Camões and Brazilian literature, will be there, real 'bambas do bairro!' ["Big cheeses in Academia"]. Go figure, our wily, cunning director of research here at the Casa, Professor Thieirs, convinced them that the language of the 'Literatura de Cordel' is the best example of the language of the masses (thus related to Philology) and convinced all these snooty professors to include a session on 'Cordel.' So that, Miguel, is where you come in. Professor Thiers remembers all your hard and good work in 1966, 1967 and 1969, so thus the invitation. Varig has communicated with us that you received the letter, and in fact are coming. All the girls here at the Casa are excited that you are still an eligible bachelor, so don't expect to be lonely after the conference meetings."

I relaxed for the first time in a while and thought, "Get ready for adventure. Off we go in an hour."

4

✦✦✦

Hitting The Lottery - Portuguese Academic Ways In Brazil

Like the Varig lady said, for not being a gambler, certainly not in Brazil's famous numbers' racket ("O Jogo do Bicho") I had "hit" the number and won the prize. So that's how I ended up writing these notes, memories and meditations on the trip that would turn into a new adventure for the "naïve gringo," ("o gringo sem jeito") in Brazil. All this plus my own "executive" decision to write it all up in "Letters" to James Hansen of the "New York Times," unsolicited upon such short notice, but always welcome (another Gaherty gamble).

At the Varig airline counter in Los Angeles, upon printing out the boarding pass the employees laughed at the situation, not making a big deal out of any of it. "Hey, go on and go, and have a good time" was their advice. There was a time of waiting, really, two; the first when no one was able to open the door on the big Boeing 747 to allow passengers in (not my first encounter with airline ineptitude, the "Letters II" reader might recall the scary fiasco in Belém do Pará in 1969 when the departing jet blew out all the terminal windows with me hunkering down like a northeastern hillbilly to escape the flying glass), and later, the heavy night fog in Los Angeles. The plane was called back to the tarmac from the takeoff strip due to the dense fog. So, all of us passengers enjoyed the incredible "on board service" of Varig seated in our comfortable seats waiting for word from the tower announcing permission to taxi and take off. It turned out great, a reintroduction to Brazilian hospitality! At mid - night there were before dinner drinks, salmon, tomatoes and eggs, French bread and cheese, chicken breast, lemon dessert, and that delicious Brazilian "cafezinho." I thought, "Not bad for starters, huh?" At two in the morning Varig took off and after five hours arrived in the international airport of Lima in Peru. Everyone left the airplane to stretch their legs and experience a bit of Lima, and after one or two Pisco Sours probably donated by the local tourist agency with the hopes of us loosening our pocketbooks for the tourist shops, once again all climbed aboard and we took off with a direct flight to Rio.

The Arrival in Rio. Much to my surprise there was someone to meet me at Galeão International Airport (I'm not a super star professor and not used to such treatment), my old friend from the Casa de Rui Barbosa, Ana Maria Barroso, the one who had sent the telegram to Varig in Los Angeles. At that point everything came together, and the "big picture" of the purpose of the trip was revealed. During the taxi ride to the hotel Ana Maria explained it all, but now in much more detail than the telegram to Varig in Los Angeles: The name of the Congress (or "Conference" as we say in the U.S.), included a euphemism reflecting Portuguese and Brazilian rhetoric - "The First International Congress on Portuguese Philology and 'The Lusiads' of Luís de Camões." How did I fit in, certainly not a Philologist or the like? It turns out there would be a session on "Popular Literature in Verse" (the academic name for "A Literatura de Cordel" in those days, a correct and very accurate name indeed), the "Cordel" being housed in the Philology Sector of the Research Center of the Casa de Rui Barbosa.

The above is all a very complicated story, another of Brazil's big "accidents." I think the only way for an entity dedicated to the life and works of the intellectual, writer, "polyglot" and statesman Rui Barbosa to have a collection of the "Literatura de Cordel," had to be a Brazilian "jeito" ["arrangement"]. "A Literatura de Cordel" was a literature extremely looked down upon in those years, so Professor Theirs and colleagues came up with a cunning idea - the "Cordel" in fact does represent the "popular language of Brazil" of the Northeast. Get it? It in effect brings the language of the masses to the Philology Sector, the sector on the study of Language! I talked a bit of this before.

SUGAR LOAF FROM THE HOTEL GLÓRIA

The taxi took me to the conference hotel, the old and famous "Hotel da Glória" in the district of the same name in the old part of downtown Rio. The taxi ride, in very early morning after a semi-empty "Galeão," Rio's international airport, was once again a revelation – the extreme poverty of the North zone and its industry and "favelas," the old torn-up Avenida Presidente Vargas, and then the slick skyscrapers in the business district of Avenida Rio Branco. The latter, the wide thoroughfare of Rio Branco, passed through the main business, banking and cultural center of the city; it was totally torn up for the construction of Rio's new subway. Brazil was in a frenzy of modernization at the time and Rio could not fall farther behind the "Locomotive of Brazil," the huge metropolis of São Paulo which already sported a large subway system. At the end of this famous avenue was the sea and around the corner was the old residential section of Glória with the famous hotel and church dating back to Portuguese royalty, specifically to the Prince Regent Dom Pedro II and the Braganças and the Empire in the 19th century.

I was exhausted, suffering jet lag, and was trying to get used to this metropolis. That did not keep me from walking down to the mezzanine and taking in one of the great aspects of the Hotel Glória - a large salon dedicated totally to Emperor

Dom Pedro II with beautiful paintings of him, Portuguese blue tile scenes – azulejos -, colonial furniture of the times, a real sight to admire (it made me think of Dom Pedro's museum in Petrópolis outside of Rio). On the other hand, there was, for the times, a bit of a "doubtful" side to the hotel: it was known as the site of the famous "Transvestite Ball" of Rio's carnival, at least that was its fame in 1971.

This was the scene. The hotel would house and host the "elite" of the Portuguese and Brazilian academic world – the "crème de la crème" of intellectuals in Philology, Literature, and most important, experts on the Portuguese Epic Poem, "Os Lusíadas" ("The Lusiads" of Luís de Camões, by far the most famous work of literature of that nation). That first evening in the hotel's "Bar Chalaça" I was introduced to an amazing group of intellectuals – Professora Luciana of the University of Rome, Américo Ramalho, Celso Cunha, Massaud Moisés, Artur Torres, Joel Pontes, Hernani Cidade of old Portugal and the important Raymond Cantel of the Sorbonne. The latter was the intellectual who put the "Literatura de Cordel" on the map in Brazil! I, young, just a beginner, would have my baptism into the intellectual world of international congresses. I know these names won't mean a thing to the reader, but in the Luso-Brazilian academic world, they were the "big hitters."

I guess to tell the truth I would be walking a very fine line between "work" and "play," not knowing what was to come. I was still chafing over the engagement - marriage fiasco, painful as it was, and as a result all the more eager to enjoy myself now with the alternative – once again a bachelor in Rio.

5

IMPRESSIONS FROM THE CONGRESS, A HINT OF FUN TO COME

It is worthwhile to tell my impressions of the Congress (I would write a "Letter" to James Hansen of the NYT, unsolicited, but I was sure, appreciated taking into consideration my past work), portraying thusly certain interesting customs from that academic world, a world so different from that of the United States. It was Old World – New World with a European Flavor and me as a tiny footnote. Telling yet of another fact of a vibrant Brazil, and ironically, more dangerous, all good for "Letters."

The Congress - the "Solemn Session" – the Opening

It all took place in the auditorium of the Rectory of the School of Letters of the Federal University of Rio de Janeiro in Niterói, Rio's sister city and "poor cousin" across the Bay of Guanabara. The first thing was of course the singing of the Brazilian National Anthem. For the reader who does not know it, the anthem is extremely lengthy, complicated for the English or North American ear, and yes, a bit funny. All the intellectuals in all their finery, dark suits, white shirt, tie, cufflinks, polished shoes, in short, immaculate, seemed to bounce up and down with the rhythm.

Then came the first orator. It was "The Cadillac" (a local joke because like the car he showed up everywhere, perorating, uttering grand seemingly "baroque" speeches) Pedro Calmon, a famous Brazilian historian from the crown prince of Brazilian locution, Salvador da Bahia, deserving of the attention of all. Humor aside, I have to confess that I owe a great personal debt to him for it was he who planted the intellectual seed for one of my projects in Brazil, this because of his own very modest book of years ago, "History of Brazil in the Poetry of Its People" ("História do Brasil na Poesia do Povo"). The volume treated popular poetry and history just before the advent of "Cordel."

The lunch or mid-day meal to follow. This is an entire lesson for the foreigner on Brazilian culture and life - the mid-day meal in Brazil in those days was the "almoço," in fact the main meal of the day. At the congress it was not one of those "cardboard" tasteless poor lunches at academic meetings in the United States. It took place in a Brazilian "steakhouse" or "churrascaria" in the neighborhood (think of "Fogo de Chão" or maybe Rio's "Porcão"). There was all manner of salad, french fries, manioc flour, and the main attraction – all possible cuts of beef, pork, and chicken. It was followed by ice cream and an excellent "cafezinho." (I will not go into a long description of the "churrascaria," but you get the idea.) The problem was, as also is the Brazilian custom, and I love the Brazilian saying, "Tudo foi regado" ("All was irrigated") with an opening "caipirinha," the Brazilian national sugar cane "depth bomb" drink, a choice of Brazilian wines and of course icy cold Brazilian draft beer. Not thinking of the consequences, I participated fairly moderately in the draft beer. The result was the afternoon session rewarded me with terrible drowsiness and perhaps a short nap or two during the proceedings. I assure you I was not alone. Heads nodded among the participants that afternoon.

During the "almoço" I met more of the intellectual "crème": Gladstone de Mello, a famous Brazilian philologist, and two wonderful colleagues of "Cordel" research in Brazil," Théo Brandão, a nationally known folklorist (in my mind second only to the great Luís da Câmara Cascudo of Natal) and Sebastião Nunes Batista, research colleague and friend at the Casa de Rui Barbosa from the late 1960s.

Impressive for the young North American in the session that afternoon was that the large auditorium was jam packed, not an empty seat to be had. I calculated some five hundred persons in the audience. This would never but never occur at an academic congress in the United States, and beyond that, I discovered that the audience <u>paid to attend!</u>

Speaking of that, during the long afternoon, a pretty young lady from the Casa de Rui dressed in a conservative black skirt and white blouse, both not hiding her charms (I had seen her often at her desk in the "Cordel" library during past research), came to my chair in the audience and handed me an envelope. It was full of bank notes, national money, I think about five hundred cruzeiros (the Brazilian "dollar" of the times). Even considering rampant inflation, it was a significant amount of change which would end up paying for small purchases, beer or soft drinks, taxis, or extra meals. The young lady explained that it was "walking around money." Jeez! ("Nossa" in the parlance of the times in Brazil!) The tradition of the honorarium for the principal speakers in U.S. congresses, notwithstanding, would never be paid in a white envelope full of cash in the middle of the congress! You're thinking "payola," no, not relevant here. In my brief career at the University of Nebraska, just two years, regarding an annual conference, my university would pay airfare and one night's lodging and meals. What I have described is Brazil in 1971, in that country of the "Third World" during economic development. I can't explain it and why should I complain? It is indeed "small potatoes" in the larger world picture of business, government and such things most of us never see or experience. So, we the academic specialists those few days were the "privileged." "Congressistas" at that! I asked the good looking, stacked envelope girl if she might drop me a note, help me to get to know Niterói and Rio a bit and spend some of the money. A few minutes later she came by, with another "like "envelope but with her phone number and this note: "Oi Professor. It will be my pleasure to show you around and have some fun later. Beijos [Kisses], Cláudia."

An aside from that day, stuff from chats between sessions. News of "Cordel." Zé Bernardo da Silva, poet and owner of the "Typografia São Francisco" in Juazeiro do Norte with ownership of the works of Leandro Gomes de Barros and João Martins de Atayde, has died. Also deceased is Sylvio Rabelo of the Joaquim Nabuco Institute of Social Sciences in Recife. Among the best of the private collections of "Cordel" in Brazil, that of Evandro Rabelo, has been sold, I believe to an entity in Pernambuco. All the above-mentioned played roles in my original research in the Northeast in 1966-1967.

Friend, research colleague and cultural guide to the folklore of Rio de Janeiro, Sebastião Nunes Batista, at the time of the Congress, was full-time as a student at the Federal University of Rio de Janeiro, trying valiantly to obtain a university degree. This is another story to tell. Sebastião was of humble roots, one of the sons of Francisco das Chagas Batista, one of the pioneering poets of "Cordel" and colleague of Leandro Gomes de Barros, the greatest name in all "Cordel". He was a modest civil servant in the Ministry of Agriculture in Rio de Janeiro. It was through the "pull" ("pistolão") of Professor Theirs Martins Moreira of the Casa de Rui that Sebastião was guided in gaining entrance to the university, not an easy task. Sebastião told me that the area of specialization did not matter, only having the degree. It was the key to the respect of co-workers in the Casa de Rui.

FERRY BOAT FROM RIO DE JANEIRO TO NITERÓI

Returning that afternoon to the hotel, the mode of transportation was the old ferry boat from Niterói to Rio with a slow and calm passage with the view of Rio – the sky line, big buildings downtown and Sugar Loaf off in the distance to the left and Corcovado with the Christ Statue to the right. I had a chance to talk to Cláudia the girl from the conference and we were just to the point of setting up a meeting that night at the Gloria when the imbecile pilot of our ferry got too close to the Rio-Niterói ferry crossing at the same time, and we actually bumped and scraped the side of the ferry. Luckily it was just that, but all of us passengers were jostled, and even old Raymond Cantel of the Sorbonne was knocked to the deck. I and Arnaldo Saraiva of O Porto were standing nearby and managed to lift him by the shoulders, shaken, to his feet. (Might have been the only way for the snobbish ole fart to recognize us young scholars!)

So, we all were okay, but I have to say that a scary image came to mind – just a few months earlier there was a ferry boat disaster in Hong Kong bay and hundreds drowned. You might say this took the "edge" off that romantic return to the ferry boat dock at Praça 15 in Rio. A Brazilian next to us on the deck laughed, if you can believe it. He said "It happens all the time. Nada de se preocupar! [Don't worry]. These captains are good buddies and like to run it close and give us all a 'thrill.'" (Hmm. Just like the "Jardim de Alah" bus jockeys to the north zone Rio market on Sundays!) The rest of the ride went smoothly, and I found myself thinking of the ferry boat scene in "Black Orpheus" ["Orféu Negro"] when Eurídice and the entire crowd on the ferry were dancing samba coming into Rio for Carnival. All the stuffy intellectuals were glad as we piled into the taxi to the hotel. You always think back, "Porra! It could have been much worse." I have to admit Cláudia was on my mind; in a quick aside after leaving the conference we had made plans to cut out of the conference two days later in Rio, go to the beach and then get to know each other.

There was another surprise that night. I was alone in the Bar Chalaça after dinner when, can you guess it, none other than Heitor Dias of the DOPS and all those past memories from the last two times in Rio showed up. Dressed in the wrinkled white linen suit, narrow black tie and a straw Fedora, he smiled, came over to the table, gave me a big embrace and handshake, saying, "Oi Miguel! De novo em nossa terra! ["Hello Mike, once again in our land"]. Hey, a big change of scene and fortune! The Hotel Glória is our most historic, although I can tell you some stories about the bull shit scenes that go on here the night of the Transvestite Carnival Ball! (In an aside to me he said, "Hey, I read your 'Letters' after you left Brazil, and I liked your report on the 'Historic Mansion' in Flamengo, even though you left out some important stuff!)" And he laughed, "We can still make a visit if you want." Speaking again to me, Heitor said, "I wonder how a folklore collector like you can be in the same company as these peacock big-time professors from Brazil and Portugal here at the Glória?! Porra! I can't make sense of such things, a waste of money by the government. Most of the intellectuals are leftists anyway, either that, or queers or eggheads, present company excluded!

"Hey, Miguel, I've missed you and some of our outings. You are still the best and most "simpatico" of any gringo I've ever met! Even though we have to keep an eye on you to make sure you're on the straight and narrow with all your blabbering of our politics! You and I have been through a lot including that ARB kidnapping plan of last time! We caught those bastards; they're pushing up daisies below the animal cages in the São Paulo zoo! Won't bother you or anyone else!

"Oh, and Chico Buarque is not exactly behaving himself these days. In hot water again with a couple of the latest songs. And back downtown to see General Goeldi at the Censorship board. But he seems to weasel out of any big troubles."

Heitor takes a minute, after ordering a "caipirinha," saying, "This is on you my friend. I hate to take much of your time, but my boss Colonel Oriosvaldo Ramos at the SNI [National Information Service, akin to the U.S. F.B.I.] whom you have met said you need to be apprised of some recent developments on the political and police scene. It's pretty tense around here. I'm not trying to scare you; all is well and believe me we've got these international venues well covered, no sense in getting embarrassed with more kidnappings, right? This won't take long."

Heitor proceeds to tell me of the major events of 1971, most I already knew about from the international papers at the library in Lincoln, but not all. Finally, he says, "Chega! A gente se vê! ["Enough! I'll be seeing you!"] Enjoy the intellectual bullshit and all the festivities. I'll be back in touch later in the week. Don't forget to have some fun after all this academic bullshit. We can maybe see Maria Aparecida!"

6

THE ROYAL PORTUGUESE READING ROOM AND DISTRACTIONS

Second Day of the Congress – the Session in the "Real Gabinete de Leitura Portuguesa" (The Portuguese Royal Reading Room) in Rio de Janeiro. The "Real Gabinete" is a gorgeous place. The auditorium has comfortable seats in front in the form of an oval, facing the seats is the dais itself, in a horseshoe form in different colors of Brazilian rosewood. Behind the dais on perhaps four levels are the stacks with all the books, but also in rich wood. There are spiral stairways to each level, also rich wood.

If memory serves me the session treated Luís de Camões, Portugal's main claim to international literary fame with his renowned epic poem "The Lusiads" which told of the epic voyage of Vasco da Gama and the Portuguese to India in 1497. It was during these moments of the congress that I really arrived at an understanding of and appreciating the role of the author of the "Lusiads" in the intellectual tradition of Portugal. I can say that not only did I read the work in graduate school but taught the same on one occasion in a reading and conference course to a graduate student in Nebraska.

The session began with a flowery speech by - surprise! - "The Cadillac" Pedro Calmon. Incidentally, famous professor Hernani Cidade of Portugal, elderly and deaf, was deep into a nap. And once again all began with the hilarious (at least to the North American ear) national anthem with everyone present bouncing up and down to the rhythm. There were baroque speeches by the Bahian Calmon and one of his fellow "conterrâneos" [fellow citizens] Hélio Simões, these contrasting with the pragmatic discourse, replete with facts and statistics by Segismundo Spina of the University of São Paulo. Should I have been surprised? It was the old Bahia-São Paulo stereotype.

There were other things that kept our minds from wandering – Brazilian problems with the microphone: the Brazilians were accustomed to speaking with the mouth too close to the microphone thus causing distortion and always at too high a volume. So, repeatedly, the orator would be interrupted by a "peon" from the Reading Room trying to adjust that devil of a microphone creating even more confusion and great difficulty in both giving and understanding the speech. It was such small detail that possibly kept me from falling asleep during the talks when such stuff was going on and trying not to laugh.

Another inconvenience. The bathroom in the "Real Gabinete de Leitura Portuguesa" was located directly behind the large horseshoe shaped carved speakers' podium, just a short distance from the orators' microphone. Inevitably after another of those huge mid-day meals including wine and beer, there were many "necessitados" or those in need, thus there was the constant opening and closing of the single bathroom door (it had a squeaky hinge) and worse, the sound of the loud flushing of the commode.

Many of the esteemed "consagrados" ["honored guest speakers"] fell asleep during the afternoon talks. And on the upper floors of the library, surrounding the speakers' table and podium, two or three stories high, there was constant foot traffic of those purportedly using the stacks or just hanging out, looking at the "band passing by" below. An appropriate aside: it was in these years that my now friend, the young and talented Chico Buarque de Hollanda, composed and sang many of his hit songs of Brazilian Popular Music [MPB] in the Festivals shown on national TV, and one of the best known was "A Banda", a great song epitomizing the essence of carnival in Rio, and those watching "the carnival bands pass by."

Suddenly there was a flurry of noise and activity, confusion and loud talking in the reading room. What the hell was this? It was the arrival of the ambassador of Portugal to "bless and address" the ceremony. He arrived with sirens and a police escort, all this in the middle of a "high - falutin'" speech by the esteemed Camões scholar from Germany. You can only imagine the fact that Germany and the German were not accustomed to being interrupted! But what can you do? It's the tropics! As I would learn later, and it really was nothing new and certainly nothing to be surprised about, not a big deal, it was just academic procedure and life going on in Rio de Janeiro. In a speech replete with high rhetoric, the ambassador

Mark J. Curran

himself inaugurated a bust of a statue outside the building, of whom I cannot say; he was accompanied by the "Cadillac" in the middle of it all. Thus, I survived the afternoon. It was better than a picture show! It was best to always "Keep your eyes and ears open."

That night there were drinks in the "Chalaça" Bar of the Hotel Glória. This was "academic business" with Hernani Cidade, Segismundo Spina, and Massaud de Moisés comparing academic life and practice in Portugal, Brazil and the United States. I think they were just "putting up" with the presence of the young "gringo." Amongst other things we all compared salaries and sabbatical leave policies, etc. One topic in the conversation was the writer Jorge Amado (I should have known better than to bring him up, he of past Marxist fame), but he was my favorite Brazilian writer. Hélio Simões of Salvador discoursed on Amado and cultural life in Salvador, the artist Carybé, the "afoxés" or black carnival "blocos" [samba "schools" of Salvador], and Jorge de Sena, the Portuguese poet at Brown University in the U.S.

The only other North American attending the congress was historian Thomas Skidmore, at that time at Dartmouth (he would move on and up to Wisconsin and finally to Brown in the Little Ivy League). He was probably the best known North American scholar of Brazilian Politics and History of the moment, together with E. Bradford Burns of U.C.L.A. The books of both would be invaluable to me back in the library in Lincoln.

7

"CORDEL'S" DAY IN THE SUN

Another day - The "Literatura de Cordel" Symposium at the Federal University of the State of Rio de Janeiro in Niterói. The auditorium was full to capacity, an unbelievable moment for me. The first speaker was young Arnaldo Saraiva from the University of O Porto, a casual acquaintance who was a rising star in linking Portugal's original "blind man's literature" ["Literatura de Cegos"] to Brazil's "Cordel."

Next was a short but incredibly complimentary introduction to my talk by the then director of the Research Center at the Casa de Rui, the successor to Professor Thiers Martins Moreira, Maximiano Campos. The talk went over well, albeit one of the more "academic talks:" "Influência da Literatura de Cordel em Grande Sertão: Veredas" ("Influence of the 'Literatura de Cordel' on 'The Devil to Pay in the Backlands'") by João Guimarães Rosa. This novelist at the time was considered the best of Brazil, a sort of tropical "James Joyce," and linking him to the "Cordel" was a large leap in critical speculation for the intellectual establishment, but I did it!

Then came the pragmatic, non-baroque presentation of Raymond Cantel of the Sorbonne, the "Star of the 'Speechifiers.'" And after all the talks there was a performance of singer-poets ("cantadores") who improvised verse to a delirious audience! The star was Azulão of "Cordel" fame in Rio de Janeiro from the late 1950s up until now in the early 1970s.

I found out only that afternoon after the session that a big blowout was planned in a couple of days for all the "congressistas" but to highlight "Cordel" and a big publication.

A small note: on the return that p.m. from Niteroi on the Rio-Niteroi ferry I had a chance to talk to Professor Cantel and to Professora Luciana from the University of Rome while we stood under umbrellas in one of the tropical rains. This time there were no bumps, scrapes or surprises.

8

SPLITTING THE SCENE WITH CLAUDIA, THE BEACH AND MORE

COPACABANA BEACH

Another Day. Cláudia and I "Split the Scene." I truly needed a break from academia and congresses, so had arranged with new "friend" Cláudia to have some needed "relax" as the Brazilians say and some fun at the beach. She met me at one of my old hangouts from past research trips, the "Braseiro Pé Sujo" [sticky foot barbecue] café in Copacabana with the still reasonable prices of "down home" Brazilian food and icy "choppe beer," all taken while sitting on bar stools at the counter: we enjoyed filét mignon, vegetable salad, "vinagrete" topping, french fries, icy cold beer and delicious "cafezinho." Cláudia wanted to know, "How did you know about this place? It's a hole in the wall place but famous to anyone who lives in Copacabana or even anyone in the South Zone?" I said, "I stumbled onto it just walking on the way to the beach on a Sunday afternoon, was hungry and that was that. My favorite place in Rio ever since.

We had arranged to be "beach ready," me with a sporty sun hat, tourist t-shirt, and "gringo" boxer style swim suit and towel and stuff in a beach bag, Claudia with that "top" all the Carioca women wore when going to the beach, and a big bag with all her stuff. So, we headed to the beach after the big "almoço." The beach scenery just two blocks away was better than past years: now the young ladies were in "tangas" and "fio dental" (eventually "the thong" in English but translated "dental floss bikini"). I said, "Makes a young man weak!" Cláudia said, in effect, "You haven't seen anything yet" as she slipped out of her top revealing a sensational Carioca physique – tanned from top to bottom, jet black, shiny hair and cool sunglasses propped on top, breasts that cried out for attention, a tiny waist, and a cool, sexy bottom with wonderful curved buns on the back side. Her suit was an aqua blue, matching the Copacabana waves. She said, "Que tal, professor? ["What do you think, Professor?"]. I thought you needed a 'distração' [distraction] from all that academic falderal of the past few days." Hey, we were at the beach, and all kinds of funny business goes on, so there was no hesitation in a deep kiss, and rubbing up against that voluptuous body. I grabbed a towel quickly to cover the erection, but she smiled and said, "I've got lots of girlfriends here in Rio and one of them loaned me the key to her apartment for the rest of the day. We'll go there after a swim and some sun, shower all this sunscreen stuff off, have a drink or two and you can tell me about Camões the Poet!" We both howled. We enjoyed the waves and she joined me in the rudiments of body surfing, "fazendo jacaré" ["making like an alligator!"]. After about two hours we had had it, piled into a taxi and were soon ensconced in a modest 5th floor apartment toward Pão de Açúcar on Avenida Atlântica itself with a view of the beach.

Like I said, after the disappointment, sadness and maybe a touch of anger with the engagement falling apart, at least unconsciously I was determined to make "the best of it" and enjoy Brazil's pleasure in the meantime. I guess you could say this was chapter one.

Cláudia and friends weren't rich; they were all students or working in early civil service careers like Cláudia for the Casa de Rui; the apartment was modest but nicely decorated. Her friend had posters of all the MPB music stars on the walls – Jair Rodrigues, Nara Leão, Milton Nascimento, and my guy, Chico Buarque. And the Tropicalia crowd that I wasn't so hot on. There were some bottles of Brahma Choppe beer and a bottle of Brazilian wine in the frig so we got into that as we peeled off our beach clothes. That just itself was worth the price of admission.

Reader alert: skip the next two paragraphs if you are not curious about fun in Rio. They will not appear in "Letters."

The dental floss top and bottom fell to the floor as Cláudia dragged me into the shower. She expertly untied my swim trunks, peeled off my shirt and began to lather both of us up. It was a little unwieldy since my now much enlarged tool got in the way. Claudia bent down, kissed it, promised more to come as she pulled me and my lips closer to those outstanding breasts. (I thought, damn! do all these Brazilian women look like they've been good customers of Rio's famous plastic surgeon Ivô Pitanguy?) We were both breathing hard by now when she proceeded to insert my tool into her very comfortable, warm vagina. I managed to protest – "Hey I'm not using a 'preservativo' (the really funny word Brazilians used then for a condom). Cláudia said, "No problem; it's all taken care of; all of us are on your Uncle Sam's birth control pills direct from the pharmacy and I made sure I took mine before today. Besides, we'd make a beautiful baby together. Mike, don't worry, it's a 'piada' (joke)."

It had been a long time, so after just a few thrusts old toolie burst its goodies. She kept thrusting until she suddenly moaned, biting my lip in the process. "O' professor, você me encheu de alegria." ["Oh, professor, you filled me with happiness"]. I pulled out and she bent over and began caressing toolie again and did god knows something with her fingers and lips and pum, orgasm again! She laughed, said, "Chega" ["Enough"]. Let's finish bathing, dry off and have some drinks and get to know each other better."

We spent the rest of the afternoon telling each other's stories. Cláudia's father worked at the Bank of Brazil in Minas (Belo Horizonte), her mom ran an upscale dress shop in downtown Belo, two brothers and a sister still lived in Minas, she being the only one ready to leave for "the big city." She had a degree in Brazilian Literature and Library Science from the P.U.C. [Pontifical Catholic

University] in Rio and was doing an internship at the Casa de Rui since it was one of the most famous libraries in Brazil, getting in via some good connections from professors from the PUC. (I had to wonder what she did to get those letters of recommendation). She said the minute she laid eyes on me in the fifth row of the auditorium she knew that this was going to happen!

I was not one to lie or bullshit anytime, so no reason to start now. I told her of my background, the time at Georgetown, Fulbright research in Brazil, the Ph.D. job at Lincoln, Brazil connections with Ariano Suassuna and now Chico Buarque for research on "Cordel" and his music. No need to fill in details of Cristina Maria, DOPS' problems or such. I did say I was serious with an American girl, a coed from Georgetown, and we had planned on marriage but that had all blown up. Cláudia seemed to perk up at that point, even though she did just kiss me and say, "Eu compreendo" ["I understand"]. Turns out she had a similar breakup in Minas before making the leap to get out of town, away from him, and to the PUC, in this case his two-timing her when things were supposed to be serious.

I said, "Look, I'm just here for two weeks, it's all business at the Congress and with Chico later, and then back to work in Nebraska. So, we can have our fun with no strings attached or obligations, right?" She smiled and said, "Sim, that's probably the way it will turn out. But we've got to have one 'date' before you leave – after that big blow out party at the Casa de Rui at the end of the congress. But I'm cool about it; we can dance a time or two and get together later."

She pulled me down to her faced, kissed me again making all the pipes heat up again. "Só uma foda para "selar" o acordo e não esquecer de mim." ["Just one screw to seal the deal and not forget about me"]. It was hot sex on both our parts. Surprising to me, Cláudia jumped up, slipped into a bra, tight blouse, tiny panties and tighter slacks, rushed to the bathroom to tidy up, and then said, "After you get cleaned up and dressed, you're on your own. I'll see you tomorrow at the Congress. You'll see that I won't embarrass the scholar concentrating on his boring poets. But you can call me and see the arrangement for after the book signing party. You are going to be a very popular man!" She blew me a kiss, said, "Leave the key on the table by the divan, and lock the door on your way out."

One result of the day off was missing the outing to the residence and gardens of Roberto Burle Marx, the most famous landscape architect in all Brazil, truly a "mortal sin" due either to the ignorance of the "gringo," or the simple fact I could not take another intellectual day and more "academia." Burle Marx was of the first ecologists in Brazil and early in his career implored Brazil and Brazilians to save the

Amazon rain forest. He was a partner with Lúcio Costa and Oscar Niemeyer in the designing and building of Brasília, the Avant – Garde capital built in a hurry from 1955 to 1960. One of Burle Marx's last projects were the gardens of the "Igreja de Pampulha" in Belo Horizonte.

MOSAIC SIDEWALK OF COPACABANA BEACH

But perhaps he is most famous for the design of the plantings on Copacabana, Ipanema and Leblon beaches in Rio and the famous "mosaic" sidewalks and later the central garden of Brasília. My loss! Well, maybe not.

9

BRAZILIAN "PEACOCKS" AND A BALLROOM EVEN FOR SAMBA

Yet another day at the Congress. We all attended the lecture by the professor that impressed me as the one to "stand out" most for his manner, his eloquence and especially his personal appearance: Leodevigário de Azevedo Filho was certainly the best dressed of the congress and all its intellectual "crème." He sported a fine dark suit, an impeccable white shirt with cuffed sleeves, fine cuff links, and a handsome tie. His talent for peroration was no less impressive marking his presence in the congress.

A short but important moment was a chat during lunch with Professor José Aderaldo Castelo a luminary in the culture and literature of Brazil's Northeast, thus our common interests. I believe he was in professor in São Paulo at the USP at the time.

I found out more details of that book signing party Cláudia has mentioned. Volume I of the series of studies on "Literatura Popular em Verso" ["Popular Literature in Verse"] was scheduled to be published to coincide with the congress, and there would be a wonderful "noite de autógrafos" ["autograph party"] held in the formal salon of the Casa de Rui Barbosa with a festive atmosphere of food and drink, music, joking and laughter, some impromptu dancing and a truly momentous meeting of the "crème de la crème" of the intellectuals from the congress. I at the young academic age of thirty-two would now always be in the company of Manuel Diégues Júnior, Ariano Suassuna, Raquel de Queiróz, Arnaldo de Saraiva, Théo Brandão, Bráulio de Nascimento and Sebastião Nunes Batista by virtue of the volume of studies. The book is seminal in its early extensive studies on "Cordel" and is going to be a "classic" in the genre. My participation was due to all that hard work in the past years, research in that old tiny room for research at the Casa de Rui, painstakingly taking handwritten notes from the booklets of "Cordel," notes incidentally I used for the dissertation and first year at Lincoln. The work was appreciated by then Research Center Director Thiers Martins Moreira who on an occasion or two gave me impromptu lectures on the role of "Cordel" during the Rubber Boom in the Amazon ("SEMTA" during World War II). What most surprised me that evening were the many students who spent their hard earned "cruzeiros" on the book. I noted: "They really read these things!" Here's my take on the shindig.

It was a big party in the "salão nobre" ["ballroom"] of the Casa de Rui. In spite of all the days and months for three years off and on working in the tiny "Cordel" library, I never had the "tour" to the second and third floors of the 18th century mansion which held the Rui's library and the "salão nobre" or ballroom. The mansion was along Embassy Row in Botafogo and I guess Rui wanted to be close to his colleagues in Diplomacy at the beginning of the 20th century. I was indeed taken aback to see it all – a baroque, almost rococó, beautifully decorated room, much like I imagined the entrance hall of a European upper-class mansion. What happened in the course of the evening was a combination social moment combined with book signings of the big "studies" volume. There was also a samba band, lots of strong 'caipirinhas,' Brazilian wine, icy "choppe" beer and wonderful "tira gostos." [hor d'oeuvres]. Cláudia was right, as mentioned, there were students in line to buy the book, have me sign it, truly appreciative of my work (this in spite of the fact I was one of the "small fish" in that very big pond of writers.)

The "caipirinhas" got to me a bit, maybe all of us, but I remember dancing with most of the Casa de Rui girls, including Cláudia (they told me later I "gave a show" ["Deu um show!"] and all enjoyed it). Gringos <u>can</u> dance samba when they have had three caipirinhas! All the conference intellectuals were there plus many invited notables (and some "penetras" [party crashers]) of Rio's intellectual society, but I did not spend much time with them. There was a lot of signing lots of books before the dancing, drinking and eating took place. At one point, Cláudia sidled up, whispered, "I'll get you home in a taxi after the party." We were now becoming a "note" for the "in the know" girl friends of Cláudia, one ravishingly cute one telling me later, "Next time it's my turn."

I don't know who noticed me and Cláudia in the taxi, but I'm sure there was "mexerico" or gossip about it, but all in good nature. Brazilians expect this and were probably pleased I was having a good time. And Cláudia probably got a raise in pay for the "above and beyond the call of duty" late hours put in. I didn't mention her dress! Poured into a low-cut red sheath top with flowing skirt. She wasn't alone; all the Casa de Rui girls were "putting on the dog," even including my formal host Ana Maria, who incidentally didn't look so bad herself, even though she was a bit older than the "staff" girls. I truly don't know how often these events took place, but like I said, with the huge budget for the conference, they pulled out all the stops. I felt like I was in a royal mansion in Europe, whatever that feels like.

I won't go on about the après-party event. Instead of taking me back to the Hotel Glória, Cláudia made a stop at the same girlfriend's apartment, saying, "She's still gone, I've got the key, so why don't we have the "saideira" [goodbye drink] and you can tell me your impressions of the big party!" All the above happened, but Cláudia somehow coerced me into another of those "close encounters of the sex kind." No complaints; afterwards she took me to the hotel and said, "It's been fun. Maybe I'll see you again at the Casa when you're reading those dusty old "folhetos!" [chapbooks]. I said, "I'll look forward to it! Adeus e beijos!"

10

A FINAL PARTY – DO YOU
TIP THE BELLBOYS?

Is the reader ready? Yet another big party took place the last night of the Congress. I truly have taken pride in never having been a "name dropper" in my all brief academic career (although the preceding paragraphs may seem to contradict that), but the "cast of characters" of all this in 1971 would never be repeated. I met Afrânio Coutinho the principal master of Brazilian Literary criticism and Professor Roger Bismut of the U. de Louvain at the closing of the congress, a formal dinner at the home of the President of Xerox of Brazil in his "house-castle" in Laranjeiras. Try to imagine the scene: a tiny Brazilian taxi crammed with professors and their wives going to a party! The hosts were Sérgio Gregori and his wife, a niece of Henriqueta Lisboa of Brazilian literary fame. The house was in Parque Guinle, the property of "old money" in Rio, the place of the presidential palace before Brasília in 1960, and the family name of one of Rio's most infamous bachelors on the social scene during Carnival two years ago; no more needs to be said. I met Vianna Moog of "Pioneiros e Bandeirantes" fame and Austregésilo de Ataíde, President of the Brazilian Academy of Letters who at that moment spoke of the major move of the Academy from the old 19th century building from the times of Machado de Assis to a new, rounded skyscraper in downtown Rio. After the party, Brazil intervened once again: on the return to the hotel there was a wild taxi ride with a driver who got lost and we ended up in front of the cog train station at Corcovado, all ending with a 2:00 a.m. arrival at the hotel. No time for the Christ Statue ["Cristo Redentor"] that night!

I forgot to mention that somewhere in all these festivities there was a diversion: a "show" at the "Club Canto" in Niterói by no less than popular singer Toquinho and the famous "sambista" Clara Nunes. Who would have thought! The samba (Clara Nunes was the best!) and all the impromptu dancing like a block party at Carnival time! All the crowd was singing and dancing throughout the show, even the slightly tubby cultural attaché of Portugal José Blanc; indeed, he was not a bad dancer.

The next day we were all checking out of the hotel heading home when at the door of the hotel, Professor Hernani Cidade asked me if was a custom to tip the bellboy in Brazil? I, more of a foreigner than he, said politely he was asking the wrong person.

Maria Barbosa of the Casa de Rui had arranged for me to stay at the hotel the next week at the ridiculous "congress" rate, such a deal. The Glória's breakfast buffet was second to none, the dining room elegant, and with all that cash they gave me earlier on I had plenty of funds for taxis to Copacabana and the beach. Before I move on to other things and surprises that week, just a final note on the Congress.

I surmised there would be other congresses and beautiful moments in the professional career in Brazil, but never would these past days described be forgotten nor the cast of characters. I, young, naïve and a newcomer in the middle of it all. Most important it was a life-long lesson on the comings and goings and doings of the Lusitanian – Brazilian academic connection.

Since this whole "deal" was a spur of the moment, I have to mention I was just on a short tourist visa and did not have that all important pseudo-diplomatic visa from the INR-WHA [Institute of Research – Western Hemisphere Agency] as last time or the boost from James Hansen and the NYT. This would not keep me from writing an unrequested "Letter" to the "Times" telling of it all. This would have consequences as we shall see.

11

BUSES, PARAKEET FIGHTS AND A MENTOR FOR FOLKLORE

Important or not was the moment on the bus after the Botafogo Tunnel and headed into Barata Ribeiro in Copacabana at rush hour: the bus driver ["motorista"] lifted the floor gear shift off its place, stuck the whole thing out the window and adjusted his mirror, than clanged it back down in place on the floor and not missing a beat!

There was one small incident to report: I witnessed on the big mosaic sidewalk in Copacabana in Rio a parakeet fight (think cock fight in the American southwest or Mexico or any number of Latin countries). The birds were yellow and red; the fight lasted about ten minutes. It was, I surmise, all highly illegal, but an exchange of money took place in the crowded audience. This was the only time in Brazil I witnessed such a sight (I have told of a major cock fight witnessed in Juazeiro do Norte in 1966, a bloody spectacle indeed.)

And there was a major encounter over several hours in the "Cordel" library at the Casa de Rui and the nearby restaurant. I really got to know Sebastião Nunes Batista. He shared with me jewels of anecdotes on the old "Literatura de Cordel." He conversed telling of his father Francisco das Chagas Batista, perhaps the "Cordel" poet who wrote the best of the long "histórias" or "romances" over the bandit Antônio Silvino, being a contemporary to his times. And Sebastião told of Leandro Gomes de Barros, the foremost poet of "Cordel" and a person who liked his "cachaça," arriving "home," a bit "tight" from it all. He mistook his way and walked into the door and house of neighbor Chagas, adding one more chapter to

33

the lore of the aforesaid poet. Only Sebastião could have told the story, his father a firsthand witness to the fact.

Sebastião told of his own life: growing up in Paraíba state, then working on the railroad in Bahia state where he had an encounter with the feared bandits of the times ("os cangaceiros"). Then came a time when he made a living under the guise of being a veterinarian in the backlands, by virtue of the great knowledge he had of livestock. And, more apropos today when he was the "Letter Writing Man" ["O Homem das Cartas"] or the "Secretary of Correspondence" at the Central Train Station in Rio de Janeiro (his real life role portrayed by the great actress Fernanda Montenegro in the internationally acclaimed Brazilian film "Estação Central" ("Central Station"). Sebastião became "the man with the typewriter" writing letters for the hillbillies at the northeastern fair of São Cristóvão in Rio (One recalls a famous Mexican film with no less than Cantinflas playing a similar role, hilariously portraying the role with his double entendre and funny dialogue). As mentioned elsewhere, Sebastião became invaluable as an informant of the "Cordel" but really of Brazilian folklore at the august research center of the Casa de Rui, and I was so fortunate to share a small part of his life. He took me to other folkloric places in Rio, including to a session of Umbanda; I never made it to the "gafieira" or popular dance hall with him but sorely missed my chance at a real part of Carioca life.

12

A Reunion With Chico And Marieta – Songs Of Protest

All I've mentioned was important, but the "main course" was an entire week spent with Chico Buarque de Hollanda and wife Marieta and all that happened during that next week. Chico and I had talked on the phone a couple of times in the spring of 1971, but he had no idea I was back in Brazil. I called and got a taxi to his place Sunday morning right after the Congress closed. Truly I was welcomed like an old friend and Marieta treated me the same although it was our first meeting. There was so much to talk about, but before all that I took too much time telling of Molly, our engagement and the falling out. Chico gave me a big "abraço" [embrace], but then smiled and said, "So you're 'legal' for some fun, not being an old married man." I did say that indeed that was the case.

Chico, with that intellectual pedigree from his family, wanted to know all about the Congress asking for a blow by blow account. I told him it had come with interesting "entertainment" sidelines but said that could wait. Marieta said "You've got to stay for dinner and maybe even more time this evening. Topa? [Okay?] "How can I refuse! It's an honor." Even though I had pretty good Portuguese, Chico talks fast and for some reason is hard for me to get everything; not so Marieta, clear as a bell. So, the main word was "Devagar por favor" ["Speak slowly, please"].

"Miguel, we've got a lot to catch up on. You are quite aware that things have gotten a lot worse this year with President General Garrastazu Médici and Institutional Act 5 (the reader recalls I wrote about this earlier). There is real fear in our daily lives now, and those of us in MPB [Brazilian Popular Music] are watched closer than ever. Oh, by the way, I want to thank you again for the accurate and flattering report you did on my songs 'Pedro Pedreiro' and 'Apesar de Você,' including our interview in your 'Letters' for the NYT in 1970. I think it helped sales! I'm jumping around with all the news and stuff I want you to hear, a lot to catch up on. Before I forget with all we have to talk about, I want to mention you should call Cristina Maria and tell of our encounter. She is after all responsible for our meeting and friendship. There is some news about her and Otávio.

"What you need to know is that the only way I can keep my sanity is to keep composing, doing concerts when I can, and mainly thinking up ways to 'Driblar a censura' ["Fool the censors"]. There are two new songs, fresh out, giving us all headaches. Things have not turned out exactly as promised as we had hoped for since getting back to Brazil. My former 'fans' who labeled me the 'unidade nacional' [national unanimous singer-composer] before Italy now say I have 'caved' to the regime. Things in fact got worse with the censorship laws and two songs in particular have complicated life now in 1971, 'Construção' and 'Deus Lhe Pague'."

"Chico, I'd like to hear them and maybe write of them, all with your approval of the text, and send it in a new 'Letter' to James Hansen in New York." Chico said, "Always better to do it now; I never know what the next day will bring. Don't worry; we can take the time now; I'll put the CD on because the totality of these songs has to be heard with our instrumental backup. I personally think I aced it, really hitting the nail on the head of what's happening now in all Brazil. There's an interesting twist. I was so fed up, really exasperated with the harassment of 'Censura Prévia' ["Prior Censorship"] when 'Construção' was being held up by the Federal Police in Brasília for what seemed like forever that I decided to ask them to prohibit it! Caught by surprise, they approved it! (a peel of laughter from Chico). Let's listen; both songs are tied together in the recording."

We listened to the recording with the pounding background rhythm (imitating the sound of a jack hammer on a construction site). Here are the four allowed lines of each, in Portuguese and English providing the flavor of them.

> Chico's "Construção"
> Chico's "Construction"
> Amou da vez como se fosse a última ...
> He made love that time like it was the last ...
> Subiu a construção como se fosse máquina ...
> He climbed the construction scaffolding like he was a machine ...

Amou daquela vez como fosse máquina ...
He made love that time like he was a machine ...
Morreu na contramão atrapalhando o tráfico.
He died on the one-way street screwing up the traffic.

The text of "Deus Lhe Pague" ("May God reward you") is interwoven with "Construção."

Deus Lhe Pague. 1971
"May God Reward You"
Por esse pão pr'a comer, por esse chão p'ra dormir ...
For that bread to eat, for that ground to sleep on ...
Pela piada no bar e futebol p'ra aplaudir ...
For the jokes in the bar and "futebol" to applaud...
Por essa praia, essa saia, pelas mulheres daqui ...
For that beach, that skirt, the women around here
Deus Lhe Pague.
May God reward you.

What Chico was saying in the entirety of the two songs was much more, an incredibly sophisticated condemnation of daily life in Brazil in 1971, first in a surreal, poetic, avant-garde song-poem using a construction site and worker to tell his story. All the verses are intermixed in succeeding strophes, adding an entirely different tone and meaning. I'll paraphrase his story. It doesn't do it justice, but you get the idea.

The construction worker makes love to his wife, kisses her, kisses each of his children, and with a timid step crosses the street to go to work. At work he climbs the scaffolding, machine-like, uses brick to build four solid walls, brick by brick in a magical design, the entire time his eyes full of tears and cement dust. He sits down to rest as though it were Saturday, eats his rice and beans like he was a prince, drinks and sobs like he was a shipwrecked sailor. He dances and shouts as though he were hearing music, and he stumbles into the sky as though he were drunk, and he floats in the air like a bird. He ends up on the ground like a paper bag, he agonizes in the middle of the Public Walkway, and dies in the street screwing up the traffic flow.

As mentioned in the above text, between choruses of "Construção" Chico sings the verses of "May God Reward You," already cited. Paraphrasing once again, this is his story, a tongue in cheek play on the age-old phrase beggars in Brazil use to thank passersby for the coins and small alms they receive, all with great irony.

He thanks God for his daily bread, a place to sleep, a birth certificate, a concession to smile, for being able to take another breath, for existing. For the pleasure of crying, the joke in the bar, the "futebol" game, for the daily news on crime, for a samba to distract. For the pleasures of daily life – the beach, the women, for the too quick love making, the shave, and off to work. For Sunday which is beautiful with its TV soap opera, mass and comics in the paper. For the "cachaça" he has to swallow, for the cigarettes, the smoke that makes him cough, and for the scaffolds, precarious, that he falls from. For one more day, agony, to put up with and get through; for the gnashing of teeth, for the noise of the city, for the demented shout that helps him to flee it all. And finally, for the professional wailing banshee woman who praises us, for the flies that kiss and cover us, and the final peace that comes and redeems us.

Not exactly pleasant like listening to a simple samba, the two songs highlight for me the real misery the dictatorship has brought to Brazilians. Chico really had little to add. "The songs tell it all. Most amazing the Censorship let them fly. Dozens of thousands of copies selling like hot cakes this summer. And now the Federal Police have figured it out and are confiscating the CDs, closing the recording studio and hauling me in again to explain. I'm not worried; there is absolutely nothing about the government, the Generals, all the imprisonment and torture going on today. There's just the daily life of the construction worker who falls to his death in the street (not that uncommon in Brazil) and what most people deal with daily."

"Chico, with your permission I'll write my 'Letter' including the text, paraphrasing of course, and your comments and send it to the 'Times.' I'll show you the text as early as tomorrow. Okay?" "Topo. ["I agree. So be it.] I trust you Mike and you've never failed me. Go for it."

13

BRAHMA CHOPPE BEER, PITÚ CACHAÇA AND ROCK N' ROLL

Then came one of the big delicious Brazilian "almoços," fish in delicious sauce, rare beef from the spit, Brazilian French fries, green beans, peas and lettuce and tomato salad, and "brigadeiro" chocolate for dessert along with steaming cups of sugary Brazilian demitasse coffee. We needed the latter because we were all sleepy, maybe partly because the whole thing was "irrigated" with lots of icy Brahma Choppe beer. The cafezinho revived us and I had a moment of inspiration, impulsive as it was, to bring up something new. "Chico, I know you studied English back in high school and college, and you went through a phase of messing around with American Rock - Elvis Presley and all the others. What you don't know is that at the same time, I was in high school and with an electric guitar, small amplifier and a good buddy as "parceiro" [partner], and we sang all those songs, even performing them a couple of times at school dances. I'm talking 'Don't Be Cruel,' 'Blue Suede Shoes,' and 'Heartbreak Hotel' by Elvis, 'Rock Around the Clock' by Bill Haley and the Comets, 'I Saw Her Standing on a Corner' by Little Richard and some schmaltzy stuff by Ricky Nelson like 'Poor Little Fool.' Why don't you and I tune up the guitars and sing some of them!"

Chico heehawed and said "That's been a long time ago, and Miguel, my English wasn't so hot and still isn't. Don't get on my case – I know Spanish, a lot of French and am damned hear fluent in Italian. That was high school and days with lots of nonsense. Let's open a couple more bottles of beer to loosen me up and give it a try. I've got my old electric here and a spare, let's tune 'em up and see what happens."

What happened was a hoot. In this case I guess, incredible as it seems, I was taking the lead. We played and sang (Chico remembered a lot more of the lyrics than I did), laughed and drank the afternoon away. After I said I didn't remember half the words, Chico dived into a desk cabinet and hauled out a three-inch stack of the old 1950s song sheets we used to buy for a quarter. We did Elvis's "Blue Suede Shoes," "Don't Be Cruel," "Jailhouse Rock" and "Heartbreak Hotel." Then Buddy Holly's "That'll Be the Day" and some of Chuck Berry's stuff. I remembered Everly Brothers, so we did "All I Have To Do Is Dream." I guess we played for an hour and a half, Chico's enthusiasm growing by the minute. "Porra! I had forgotten all those. What about the Beatles?" "The only one I know is 'A Hard Day's Night.' After that I 'tuned out' of American music, especially Rock n' Roll - studying Portuguese, Brazil and 'Cordel.'" (Laughter.)

It was now late afternoon and both of us were not real alert when Chico had an inspiration: "Hey, Miguel, porra! Let's record this at Philips. I can get a fine lead guitar player, drummer and pianist on board and a great female backup voice, all with a phone call. With you and me singing lead and they following and doing electric guitar background, it'll be a real 'novidade' [novelty] here in Brazil! Improvise! Merda! No one expects Chico Buarque to sing American stuff, it'll sell thousands just for the novelty. And best of all, the 'Censura' [Censorship] guys will crap having to rave about the 'Leftist' Chico Buarque doing U.S. Music. We can call it 'Mistakes of Our Youth' or maybe 'Taking a Rest from Brazil.' What do you say? No kidding, I can set this up in the studio for Friday."

"Chico, merda, I'm an amateur, but I've done these songs dozens of times in the late 1950s in the band room in high school with a good buddy harmonizing. And there's no reason for you to know I did a spur of the moment show in Campina Grande and later the 'Veleiro' in Recife in 1967 playing the same stuff. A guy in Campina pulled a knife on me after the 'show' in Campina Grande, saying Paraiba didn't need any more gringo imperialism! Friends calmed him down and basically told him to go home and sleep if off. Gossip in Campina the next day was about the 'gringo' who put on a show ['deu um show'] in that small-town night club. But that shit was still by an amateur and fueled by 'choppe.' Oh, a worry on my part: we're brainwashed in the U.S. What about the copyrights?"

"Não se preocupe! [Don't worry!] All this old Rock n' Roll is almost 20 years old now, and besides we have a standard general permission for U.S. songs, part of the 'friendship agreement' your country is instigating with our generals to fight the communists! No holds barred and all restrictions waived! Não diga mais! Donc deal! I'll take care of everything, instruments, lyrics and song sheets, the backup buddies, a lady harmonizing and we can do it in six hours at Philips on Friday, two for rehearsal and four of recording. Hey, nobody will expect a smooth professional job on this; I'll bill it as a kind of joke and make a big deal that we were all just starting out to learn music. 'Mistakes of Our Youth.' I like it! In fact, that was the case; I could scarcely play the guitar and you'll see my English has this, uh, heavy accent! You are in deep trouble if you back out. Nossa, it's like reliving São Paulo and the high school years in the 50s! What a hoot!"

14

An L.p., Fun And Success And The General's Approval

I don't know if it was all that beer that started it, Chico "escaping" from the tension of 1971 or what, but we pulled it off. That Friday I was with Chico up in the Alto da Boa Vista at the Philips Recording Studio. We met his regular drummer, backup guitarist pianist, a genius on saxophone, and Gini, a terrific singer who not only knew English but could harmonize in the right places. Amazing! I had never been around real professionals and realized how quickly they could improvise, rehearse and put together an amazing final product.

Chico opened with a folksy monologue telling of his days as a student at the "colégio" [high school] in São Paulo and a teenage "loucura" [craziness] for American Music, Rock n' Roll, especially Elvis Presley, all this before he was turned on by João Gilberto, Tom Jobim, Vinicius and others to Bossa Nova, and the rest was history.

We had a song list, no introductions to each tune other than Chico's voice with a one-liner, then "Bam!" An instrumental intro with an amazingly close rendition of the original (these people knew all that music, like Chico from their teens), a signal by Chico to all us singers to "come in" and then a verse or two and a chorus, and on to the next tune. We rehearsed for two hours and then "went live." It went something like this:

Chico: "Elvis Presley"
"Blue Suede Shoes:"

42

Well, it's one for the money! Two for the show! Three to get ready!
And go, cat go.!
Don't you, don't you step on my Blue Suede Shoes! ...
Burn my house, steal my car, do anything you want to do,
but don't step on my blue suede shoes."

"Heartbreak Hotel"
Well, since my baby's left me, I found a new place to go,
It's down at the end of lonely street, near Heartbreak Hotel.
I getta' so lonely baby, I getta' so lonely baby
I getta' so lonely I could cry.

All this was followed by "I'm All Shook Up" "Don't Be Cruel," "Jailhouse Rock,"
and a schmaltzy "Love Me Tender."

I haven't yet said that the entire session was heavily "irrigated" by Brahma
Choppe Beer and "cachaça." Everyone howled between takes. I insisted we do
Buddy Holly even though Chico said he only knew just a bit of "That'll Be
the Day."

"Well, that'll be the day, that'll be the day, that'll be the day, Until I die."

We did a really corny, lousy rendition of the Everly Brothers' "All I Have to Do
Is Dream:"

When I want you, in the night,
When I need you, with all my might,
Whenever I want you,
All I have to do is dream, dream, dream, dream, dream, dream. ...

The session ended with some of the black music from those days, Little Richard
and Chuck Berry. The Brazilians really got into this, especially, Gini, a beautiful
Carioca mulatta who said she had a stack of the old 45s and 33s back at home in her
apartment in Flamengo.

It's Saturday night and I just got paid! ...
Goin' to the dance and I can't be late!
Gonna rock it up! Gonna rip it up!
Gonna rock it up! At the ball tonight!

And,

> "I saw her standin' on the corner. A yellow ribbon in her hair!
> I saw her standin' on the corner! Lookie there, lookie there, lookie
> there!
> I said "a young blood," I said "a young blood" I said "a young blood"
> I can't get you out of my mind!

We didn't do any more because we couldn't remember any more, and by that time were too far gone if we did know more. It worked out to a "long play" with ten tunes, five to a side. Chico stuck with his original album title "Mistakes of Our Youth" but insisted on a photo of all of us on the cover. The producer yelled from the booth, "A Take! Not up to our usual. But a take!"

I would only hear from Chico later what would happen. The album hit the streets, Chico's thousands of fans got the joke, but starved for anything from him, lapped it up. And sales were in the tens of thousands. And no surprise, General Goeldi of the "Censura Prévia" waxed enthusiastic, telephoning Chico, I'm including the original Portuguese, after all, talking of a phone call from the President of Brazil to General Goeldi:

> "Ótimo, rapaz! E' uma maravilha para nossas relações exteriores com os EUA. Até o Garrastazú Médici me telefonou 'babando' sobre a boa publicidade. E, não deixe de cumprimentar o Mike Gaherty. Querer ou não, será já conhecido em todo o Brasil. Querido e não esquecido!"

> "Great, kid! It's marvelous for our foreign relations with the U.S.A. Even Garrastazú Médici phoned me, practically dripping with enthusiasm over the good publicity. And don't forget to congratulate Mike Gaherty. Like it or not, he will now be recognized all over Brazil. Beloved and not forgotten!"

15

A BRAZILIAN NICKNAME, THE PAECAMBU CONCERT AND THE DOPS

There was another side to that coin: Chico's former fans on the Left used it for fodder that once again Chico had "sold out" to the Military to get back into Brazil, and the U.S. Rock n' Roll album was proof! There were two or three concert dates canceled when protesters with signs of "Vendido ao Tio Sam" ["Sold Out to Uncle Sam"] appeared outside the venue gates, this happening in Recife and Bahia. For some reason Rio and São Paulo folks did not mind; everyone knew Chico's story from São Paulo and high school days, so as he said, "Foda! ["What the f***!"] Let's reminisce!" He wanted me to join him and the band on the road to Paecambu Stadium in São Paulo and a concert and to sing a couple of "Mistakes" songs, but I said my visa was soon to expire. Chico said, "I have friends who can fix all that. Vamos, 'Arretado,' ["Awesome"] Live a little!" The reader may know Chico was famous for inventing and using nicknames for his friends, even from the old days in high school, so this was par for the course and a thrill for me.

After a call to some high-falutin' person at Itamaraty (the Brazilian State Department), I was told to appear with passport at their office in Rio where a new visa was stamped into the passport – this time for one year with "researcher, journalist, scholar and musician" stamped as to user.

It was a whirlwind; I found myself on a Varig charter flight with Chico and his band two days later to São Paulo. Right after landing we were hustled in a "kombi"

[Volkswagen bus] to the stadium, incidentally most famous for the leftist students and Brazilian history as the place Luís Carlos Prestes "O Cavaleiro da Esperança" ["The Knight of Hope"], a title invented given to him by writer Jorge Amado, gave his "return" speech to Brazil after being exiled in the 1940s as a Communist. After a rehearsal and "warm up" of "choppe," "erva" ["weed"] and "cachaça," me too nervous and afraid to touch the grass and be affected much by it, but "into" the "choppe," the doors were opened, fans streamed in, all singing Chico's songs. We hit the stage before 15,000 fans; Chico said we would open with three or four songs from the "Mistakes from Our Youth" album. We sang "Blue Suede Shoes," "Don't Be Cruel," and "Peggy Sue" to standing applause and cheers before Chico launched into the regular stuff including "Deus Lhe Pague" and "Construção." He introduced me as a new friend, and more importantly, a "friend of Brazil," a college professor and NYT writer plugging his stuff in New York, but as Brazil's "major scholar on the "Literatura de Cordel,'" and Chico used his now familiar nickname for me, "Gringo Arretado" ["Awesome Gringo"]. He then sang "Pedro Pedreiro." Huge applause.

I had talked before a couple of hundred kids in my high school days, introducing assemblies as Student Council President, another few hundred at a variety show at Georgetown when my buddy and I did a parody on a sappy country western radio program, and the recent talk at the Philology Congress in front of 500 folks, but was unprepared for all this. The crowd standing on their feet were shouting "Arretado, Arretado" until I took a bow and exited the stage. Later from backstage I heard the thunderous applause for Chico's "musical commentary" on Brazil. I had never attended a big MPB live show and had no idea how raucous it could get. The beer and cachaça were flowing backstage as we watched Chico wow the fans. And it all was pretty cool until the side door leading to the backstage suddenly banged open, and a half dozen military armed guards of the DOPS [Department of Public Security] with rubber night sticks in their hands led by a fellow in a black suit and thin tie barged in. Off stage, he said to all of us, "Stay put. Produce your documents. This is the end of the party."

He then walked immediately over to the stage manager and ordered him to cut the sound to the band and figure out a way to get the fans out of there. The stage manager announced on the one live microphone something like "Due to unforeseen circumstances, we have to cut the show short. Your money will be refunded. Please file out slowly to the box office, and in short order you will receive the refund. Thank you in advance for your cooperation."

Ha! Bedlam broke loose! Imagine 15,000 fanatical fans of Chico, most by now "loosened up" with quantities of Brazilian beer, "cachaça," and "erva," and their reaction to the announcement. Programs, chair cushions, beer bottles, all were thrown into the air and up on to the stage. Chico and the band, now without microphones, sang "Construção" and "Deus Lhe Pague" again, and were drowned out by the audience singing along with the same lyrics. God, it was an unforgettable moment, this was the real Brazil.

The master of ceremonies came out on the stage again, now facing a raucous crowd, nearly out of control. He repeated his message of a refund and would the audience please file out to the many "guichês" [cashier cages] of the box office. He motioned to Chico to leave the stage, looking back to the armed guards backstage. Just then a few of the most rabid fans began approaching the stage, trying to climb up the six-foot-high wall. When the first were crawling over the stage lights, the military police went into action, rushing forward with belly clubs and whacking them on the arms, shoulders and some on the side of the head, pushing them back down to the orchestra floor. Chico yelled, "Pára com isto seus bestas! ["Stop this you animals!]. They are just reacting to the stopping of our music. Turn the power back on, we'll play a last tune, and things should calm down." Amazingly enough the police captain agreed, the master of ceremonies turned on the juice, and Chico shouted out to the crowd, "O' gente, Calma. Vamos cantar 'a despedida' e ir p'ra casa." ["Okay, everybody, calm down. Let's sing the last song and go home."] He and the band launched into "Apesar de Você" ["In Spite of You"] and the applause was delirious. Even though the song was prohibited by the "Censura," the stage manager and the police chief had the good sense to let it go on, verse after verse. Finally, Chico took the microphone for the last time and said, "O' gente. Somos de paz. Lembrem deste momento, a alegria e a energia de nossas canções! Não esqueçam deste momento. Obrigado e até a próxima." ["Friends. We act in peace. Remember this moment, the happiness and energy of our songs! Don't ever forget this moment. Thank you until next time."]

The crowd roared but began to file to the exits of the huge stadium, convinced by their hero that this was indeed the best stance at the moment. Chico walked off stage, the guitar strap still around his shoulder, rubbing his chin where a bottle or a club had landed a blow with a subsequent large, red bruise, and said to the DOPS officer,

"Por enquanto, vocês mandam. O próximo encontro e momento talvez seja nosso! Obrigado. Somos de paz. A gente vai juntar o equipamento, botar nos caminhões e nós de kombi ao Guarulhos. Mas, há a questão do cachê. Acredita ou não, a gente não vive só de aplauso."

"For now, you are in charge. The next encounter and moment may be ours! Thank you. We're going in peace. Let us get our equipment together, pack it into the equipment truck and us into the kombi to Guarulhos Airport. But there is the question of the 'cachê' [performance fee]. Believe it or not we don't live just on applause."

The stage manager assured Chico he would be getting a check in Rio the next day. Chico said, "Certo, mas, conheço esta manobra. Se nao receber, não haverá' outro concerto aqui." ["Certainly, but I'm familiar with this maneuver. If I don't get it, there will never be another concert here."]

Chico told me on the way to the kombi after equipment was packed and all was in order to leave, "Miguel, this has happened before. It's the 'macacos' [gorillas] way of just reminding us that they are in charge. They've okayed our flight back to Rio and with one proviso – go home, act like nothing has happened, no interviews to the press and our office in Rio will be in touch." He laughed, a bit sardonically I thought, rubbed his sore chin, patted me on the shoulder and said, "Hey I promised you some excitement last year when you would return to Rio. Just not quite what I had in mind. This has been a lot more fun. Porra! They'll be talking about this and writing about it for a long time. I think it's all going to get pretty sticky for all of us, you, me, the band, but also DOPS. Manhandling people from the audience and threatening a person with your credentials, passport and visa can be embarrassing. 'A Folha de São Paulo' and 'O Globo' will report it all, and puxa, [damn] maybe even the 'Times' will pick it up and do an article. Expect for us to be back downtown to explain ourselves next week. But I've got some ideas, strategy and a cunning plan – we'll get together at the house, get our stories 'straight' and go downtown together. I suggest you call Cristina Maria before next week; you may not get another chance before all hell breaks loose." He laughed again, saying, "Arretado, I'm going to take good care of you. Calma! Tranquilo! You may want to get on a plane and get lost in the Nebraska library (assuming they have one, ra ra ra) for a while after this."

16

AN ACCOUNTING AND HEITOR DIAS

Back in Rio it turned out as Chico predicted. Along with all those warm fuzzies for "Mistakes of Our Youth" from the past few days, the shit hit the fan for Chico and secondarily for me, small as my part was in the whole thing. It all had to do with the continued crazy fan support for "Construção" and "Deus Lhe Pague," my "Letter" to the "Times" along with the interview and explanation of it all by Chico, and the show in São Paulo. It would turn out to be "Chapter II" for me with the government censorship and the AI-5 policy. Like the DOPS guy in São Paulo had said, they would "Get in touch." But Brazil is crazy, and it wasn't all business downtown. There was a detour in Flamingo at Maria Aparecida's place, explained by what came next.

The first sign of trouble in Rio was, you guessed it, an unexpected encounter with old DOPS "friend," Heitor Dias. It was just a day after "Mistakes of Our Youth" hit the stands with all the falderal. I was leaving the apartment building in midafternoon and there was the black car, Heitor leaning against the stairway smoking a Marlboro. He stood up, came up and gave me a big bear hug and said, "Alô Miguel! I've been waiting for a chance to see you, my old U.S. buddy and partner in 'crime.' Está livre? Vamos para meu 'ponto' a tomar umas e outras e te trago 'ao dia' com as últimas." ["Are you free? Lets go to my hangout and have a few drinks and I'll bring you up to date with the latest."] A lot of water under the bridge, and it's getting kind of murky. You may need a lifeboat this time!"

"Oi Heitor! What an unexpected pleasure! Haven't seen you since the Hotel Glória a few days ago. This sounds a bit ominous, but you're in charge, I haven't eaten and am a bit thirsty at that. Let's do it."

So, his driver took us to the old "pé sujo" bar where we sat amongst a fairly raucous p.m. crowd, started with some "Brahma Choppes" in the big bottles, the appetizers and mainly Heitor's words of wisdom to me. He didn't seem to be in any hurry, saying he was off duty, for now. We ordered a light late afternoon "lanche" ["lunch"] (not for me, more like a full dinner) of "batata frita, filé, salada de alface e tomate" all with the beer glasses full (the reader may remember Brazilians can't stand to see an empty glass in front of them), and then strong "cafezinhos" afterwards.

"Miguel, you never cease to amaze me! First the women and hot sex! You're the one who should be setting me up here in Rio! That Cláudia is one sweet piece of ass! I can see why you spend so much of your time in the 'stacks' at the Casa de Rui, and I don't just mean those dusty "Cordel" booklets!" He heehawed at his own joke. "I guess I can see why they are treating you so well, jeez, a gringo amongst our egghead professors! Congratulations on all that.

"But it's what you've been doing since that interests me and my bosses. That whole damned business at Paecambu Stadium in São Paulo was just the straw that broke the camel's back. I warned you earlier on, didn't you get that? It was a warning about hanging out with Chico Buarque, in fact I told you his troubles with 'Censura Prévia' were on-going. I guess you didn't take ole' Heitor's advice eh? But, 'porra,' you seem to have had an Ace in your sleeve! Singing rock n' roll with our commie leftist friend, and on top of that a hit record! Nossa! Are you getting any royalties? You can start paying for all these drinks and food! I've got to admit, you've got a good voice and can handle a 'guitarra,' I guess I shouldn't have been surprised! 'Gringo Arretado.' If you don't tell my boss the Colonel, I'll let you know I bought one of the LPs! I'm waiting for you to sign the cover! We all liked that ole' rock n' roll, me still in my early less serious years! How's it go, 'Weel, since my beibe left me.'" He belly laughed again. "But you may need some ready cash to pay your room and board in one of our accommodations downtown, I think you get my drift.

"You will be getting a call the end of the week from Chico. Guess what? You get to meet General Goeldi again and soon. I think this time he may not be as gracious as last year. The shit has hit the fan first of all with that last 'Letter' to the 'Times' when you went too far with your hero worship and babbling about 'Construção' and 'Deus Lhe Pague.' And now you're in the middle of that brawl at the Paecambu! I know you were just the 'warm up' with the Rock n' Roll, but in the wrong company for what happened later. You better get your ducks in a row. You may wonder, why am I telling you all this ahead of time? I guess because, believe it or not, I really like you and believe your heart is in the right place. And I want you to know we're going to give you a fair shake. But Jesus! Be careful! Chico is not 'untouchable' no matter what you and he may think. We've got a revolution to run, have finally got Brazil on the right path, and we don't need any screwups. Are you getting me?"

"Heitor, thanks and thanks again. Damn, the feeling's mutual. We've got a bit of 'history' between us now. You've got to know the Rock n' Roll was just a whim at first, maybe after too many Brahmas, but was just something for fun. The other, the 'Letter,' was work, plain and simple. My job is to report on Brazil to the 'Times,' including any connection to Chico and his songs. I tried to keep it all unbiased, reporting on the facts as I knew them. I'm sorry if it rubbed some people the wrong way. I guess you're right; I'll have to be ready for the 'heat' downtown. I'm thinking, we both need some 'relax,' as you Brazilians call it, before all that stuff comes down. I guess you may be guessing what I'm getting at. How is Maria Aparecida? And the girls? Any chance we could take a break from all this today? I've got the time and the inclination. You know the engagement and Molly is old news."

17

A Reprise – The Brazilian Patron Saint

"I was hoping you might suggest that; no time like the present. It's a little early but that place is always open. Maybe we can have what you gringos call an early p.m. 'after sesta [nap] wake me upper.' Ha ha. I'll get my driver José on over here. But you'll be paying Aparecida. By the way, she takes credit cards!"

The driver picked us up and zoomed through traffic to Flamengo. He dropped us off and sped off. Heitor pushed the buzzer at the door, a voice said, "Who is asking?" and Heitor said, "An old customer, Heitor," and the door opened. A beautiful young chick let us in, said, "Come on into the living room," and we settled into the divans, no sooner seated then cold "choppes" and "caipirinhas" appeared in front of us. Then Maria Aparecida came down that incredible rosewood stairway, smiled, and greeted us. She was dressed in a skintight green gown, a slit in the side showing wonderful legs, and a low-cut top with plenty of carioca 'décolletage' to distract us. She smiled, laughed and said, "Heitor I was expecting you, but Miguel! It's been too long! She came over, planted a luscious kiss on my lips and said, "I've been waiting for you. We need to talk about Castro Alves, Gonçalves Dias and the 'Navios Negreiros' poems. And then maybe I can interest you in some of, what do you 'gringos' call it, 'foreplay, by-play, play by play,' I don't know what you call it. Heitor knows his way around this place, and so do you for that matter. Shall we go upstairs to my 'office' and get re-acquainted?"

"Maria Aparecida, we've got a lot to talk about. Lead the way."

We walked up that rosewood stairway, down the hall to her "office," you may remember from last time, entered the dark wooden door way, and walked into the "living" with all the images of literary figures from the Brazilian past to now. Maria Aparecida smiled, asked me to sit down on the comfortable divan in the living, said, "What would you like? I've got Johnny Walker Red and Black, or are you in a Brazilian mood? Caipirinhas (the best in Rio) or icy Brahma Choppe? Or even our good Rio Grande do Sul red or white? Meu Deus, it's good to see you. Miguel, you look fine. No one else here can give me the same conversation and thrill." As she said this, she snuggled close to me, let me feel the full length of that body including the warm breasts. Then she kissed me, wow, taking me to that "ready room" but held back, laughing, saying, "Plenty of time for that my friend," let's talk first.

"Like everybody else I've seen and heard 'Mistakes of Our Youth' with you, Chico and the band! What a hoot! I went right out and got an LP before the DOPS pulled them all from the stores. And 'O Globo' and Globo TV covered that whole mess at Paecambu. First of all, you're lucky to be alive and worse, not in the 'detention rooms' the DOPS have downtown. Secondly, damned if you are not some kind of a celebrity in Brazil! I'm going to have to charge double! 'Olha,'[Look], you know Heitor and I go way back, and he's the reason we met, but Miguel, he's got a job to do too. Don't cross him or think because he's your 'buddy' that nothing can happen. It can. I've seen Heitor in 'code red' ('caça de comunistas') ["the hunt for communists"] before and it isn't pretty. You may think just because I work here that I or we girls don't know what's going on. Ha! Half of our clients either are doing stuff to fool the government ['driblar a censura'] or are government guys after the 'bad guys.' I'm not quite sure where you fit in. I've seen the articles in the 'Times' including the last one on 'Construção' and 'Deus Lhe Pague.' I can tell you the censors have read it, and maybe you weren't doing Chico any favor by explaining it in prose for the 'Times's' readers. I think the 'macacos' downtown have it and you figured out."

I put my fingers to her lips and said "Whoa! ["Chega"] Lindalva! More important, how have you been? It's been a year since our 'interview.' By the way how did you like the way I described your place of business in the 'Letter'?"

Lindalva smiled, kissed me again and said, "You put us in a good light and even have brought in some new business from the foreign sector, you know, the 'filet mignon' gringo group. But I remember a lot better how we got along. What do you say we take up where we left off; you need some serious 'relax' from São Paulo." She opened a bottle of champagne, poured us generous glasses and toasted, "To your 'caralho' and my 'xibiu' and howled with laughter.

Reader Alert (like the warnings on TV); the reticent can skip this paragraph, incidentally, not for "Letters." The champagne was delicious, and better yet, Lindalva's expertise; I've said it before, my "tool" acting up in the mares' corral. We did a slow, mutual stripping down of clothes, she as exotic as ever, crawled into bed where she began to caress me and I in turn her, her nipples hardened to my tongue's touch, and then an easy inserting into her "xibiu," slow moving in and out, faster, and then "kaboom," Gaherty explodes. Lindalva says, "Don't stop moving." Gaherty gasps, "I'm in a 'downward spiral,'" but before it was too late, she groaned, said "Sim, mais! Mais!" And then she relaxed. "Miguel, você não deixou de me deixar ficar feliz. O' enxadão! Não posso explicar. Parabens." I'll leave this up to my educated reader's imagination. No translation needed.

She kissed me, rolled over and filled the champagne glasses again. She surprised me – "After you left a few months ago, I went over to the Casa de Rui, got a library card, went back into the stacks and read a couple of dozen of those "folhetos" [chapbooks] you keep talking about. So now I understand what you are up to (aside from our local gymnastics). And I'm beginning to put two and two together with Chico's 'Pedro Pedreiro' and 'Morte e Vida Severina.' It all adds up. I get it when both Heitor and Chico call you 'gringo arretado.' I could add an adjective or two, maybe "gringo enchadão," but that wouldn't be proper. So, I went back and read Ariano's 'Auto da Compadecida' and Jorge Amado's 'Teresa Batista Cansada de Guerra' and I get it! You can come and visit anytime!"

"Lindalva, I know the score and your life here. I'm beginning to not feel like a customer but a very close friend, but I'm asking you to take this 'present' I brought (Rodolfo the poet in Bahia would take my 'presents' after his interviews.)" It was a $100 bill I had stashed away for the trip.

She said, "On principle I can't take it, but with real life here, how about if we call it a 'gift' for groceries and some necessities? I can live with that. I don't need a visit to Ivô Pitganguy for plastic surgery yet, as you can tell, but 'business expenses' like cosmetics and all don't come any cheaper. But, 'porra,' we are wasting our time." She wrapped her arms around me, brought my face down to those luscious breasts, eased my tool into that warm vagina again, and we soon were sweating and breathing hard in some ardent lovemaking. After we both had 'had our way' she rolled over, said, "O' arretado, you better get back down and meet Heitor, or you'll lose your ride."

"Lindalva, you are right. It's been great. Lots of stuff to come soon. It's been great."

I dressed, went down to the main salon where Heitor was drinking a "caipirinha," smoking a Marboro, and seemed to be in no hurry. "Tudo bem? Pronto? I'll take you back to Dona Julia's, but we've got to talk 'serious' for a minute or two. Okay?"

"Fine, Lindalva and I will be in touch."

"We can talk in the car back to your place. 'Arretado,' I've got it that General Goeldi has a 'command performance' for Chico and you next Tuesday. I won't be present, but I've got some advice. Keep your mouth shut, talk only when you're talked to, be courteous and above all, be cooperative. Good words about the General himself (you can't use his name), the subdued way they are treating you, and the promise of a good report to the 'Times' might get you out of hot water. To the contrary they cannot only revoke your visa and hustle you out of the country, but an 'accidental' roughing you up might punctuate his remarks. We are experts at that, and you'll show no bruises. Porra! I wish this were not happening; we've had some great moments. And you're not a 'filho da puta gringo' or "veado" but a real 'arretado.' I have an idea I'll see you at the airport in a few days."

"Obrigado Heitor. Whatever happens I won't be forgetting all this." We embraced and he climbed in the car and sped off. I was greeted at the door by no less than Dona Júlia, a huge smile on her face, saying, "Nossa! Miguel. I had no idea I had such a famous guest. I could raise your rent, but suffice for now you just take a while, drink a Cearense [State of Ceará] 'cachaça' with me and fill me in on the details. We don't get much excitement here in the pensão [boarding apartment]. If I were 40 years younger, we'd have the conversation in bed! It's the least you can do for an old 'nordestina.' And by the way, that's a different perfume I smell all over you. What else have you been up to?"

I ignored her query. "Pois, Júlia, what do you want to know? I assume you saw the TV Globo coverage; it had most of anything going on, including bits of the concert, the melee and Chico's getting everyone to calm down and leave the stadium. We were hustled to the airport, with a police escort no less, put in a private waiting room away from any crowds and then hustled out to the airplane. I'm just getting here now after another command performance with one of my "friends" from the DOPS. I think I am in a bit of shock now and really just need a few hours' sleep. O.K.?"

Júlia agreed I looked a little for the worse, sniffed the perfume again, said, "I don't think I'm getting the entire story, but go ahead and lie down. All this activity is wearing you out! Ha ha ha. I'll fix you coffee and a snack when you get up."

After a much-needed nap of three or four hours I got up, drank Dona Júlia's café amidst more chit-chat than I wanted, i.e. "What's Chico like? How did you get mixed up in all this? We didn't know you do music, that was a hoot. Did the police rough you up?"

"Don't know what to say, more later, Dona Júlia."

18

CHECKING IN WITH THE FERREIRAS

Then I excused myself, used the boarding house phone and called Cristina Maria's house. It was now late afternoon and when she answered, all excited and laughing, she said, "You've got to come over right away this evening. We'll have drinks, a light supper, and get the story firsthand from ole 'Arretado.'" "Fine," I said, "I'll be over in an hour." This gave me time to shower, clean up, shave and make myself presentable at the Ferreira household. Dona Júlia, nosy as ever, (and probably listening in on my phone call) said, "Aha! It's the rich chick across the street. I thought you were done with her. What gives? I guess she can't resist a celebrity." I said, "Dona Júlia, I am friends of the entire family. It's just a social call." She smiled as I went out the door, "I guess you've got your key. We won't be expecting you early. And smiled again, knowingly."

The time went by fast and I was at the Ferreira's apartment. I rang the doorbell and Cristina Maria answered, opening it wide, saying "Alô Arretado! Que honra ter você em nossa casa," ["Hello cool guy! What an honor to have you in our house,"] giving me the air kisses on both cheeks and only slightly rubbing up against me. No harm done. "Come on in, everyone is really excited to hear the real story from the horse's mouth!"

The living room was jammed full – Jaime, Regina, Cristina Maria's two teen age brothers, her younger sister. I did the courtesies, shaking the hand of and embracing Regina, Christina Maria's mother, gripping Jaime's hand and the embrace. And a quick gringo high five to the brothers saying, "I thought you would have better things to do than listen to the adventures of a worn out, tired 'gringo.'" Both laughed, and one said, "We would not miss this for anything. A friggin' celebrity in our midst! All our friends at the colégio will be 'babando' ['drooling'] to hear the story."

Jaime looked older, a little thinner than last time, geez, it had been almost a year. I said, "Senhor Ferreira, how in the world are you? Last time we talked you were a bit shaky. I don't know if I did the right thing on bailing out on you and the family, but that short visit was not to avoid you, but give you all your privacy and time for you to rest after the heart attack."

"Oh Miguel, thanks for your concern. As for the heart attack, I followed doctor's orders for the first time in my life, cut way back on work, rested a lot more, cut down on the imported scotch, and did what Regina told me to! I've lost a few pounds, have more grey hair, but I'd say I am back 90 per cent! I am sure you are well informed of all that's happened these past few months, no need to get into all that right now. Your last week has been a lot more exciting than my now regular interviews with the DOPS. It's almost all pro-forma: How's business? Any trips planned? Any good contracts? Porra! With 'Ninguém segura este país' and 'O Brasil pra' frente' business has been good. Oh, one bit of news, Christina Maria can fill you in, the arrangement I had hoped for Otávio did not exactly turn out well. He's a good young man, but he came on like a lion and seemed to know more about my business than I did. I marked it off as exuberance and enthusiasm, but after a few months we both had a heart to heart and mutually decided he might have more freedom to exercise his new ideas in his Dad's firm in São Paulo. But enough of that! Let me pour you one of those scotches and you can fill us all in on these last few weeks in Brazil. I understand why you did not contact us earlier, given the situation when you left Brazil last August. Lots of water under the bridge and all that, but. Rapaz [Hey guy], the times have changed. Estamos doidos a saber de tudo! ["We're crazy to hear all about it."]

"You cannot be more surprised than I! No one could have predicted the last two months, especially the last two weeks. Not all has been happy. My planned marriage to Molly fell through; I won't say things can't change, but for now there are no plans. Not her fault. Not mine either. In a strange way, it has allowed me to begin 'anew' in Brazil, has opened up some unexpected doors, but also may cause me some grief."

I filled them in on the Philology Congress and Camões, saying how well that had worked out professionally, but none of the extra-curricular details. And

I explained since the trip was supposed to be quite short, my original visa was tourist and just for a month, no contract this time with the "New York Times" or diplomatic status in the passport. I quickly filled them in on professional matters, Ariano Suassuna and the book in Recife, the real academic boost to have been invited to the Congress. But then said, "I doubt that's why all of you are 'entusiasmados' [enthusiastic]. Here it is in a nutshell: I've been with Chico Buarque and Marieta a lot, the continued research has gone far better than I ever could have imagined. It was just kind of an accident that all the Rock n' Roll and songs in English came up.

"You've seen the news, so I'll just fill you in on my take on things. After a few drinks and working on an interview with Chico about 'Construção'" and 'Deus Lhe Pague' for a lark I brought up that I had played guitar and sung old U.S. rock n' roll and pop music back in the late 1950s. I told him I knew of his liking of the same in early days in "colégio" in São Paulo so why didn't we heat up a couple of his electric guitars and a amp and sing some of them. Chico was reluctant, I think because of his English, but I could have cared less so we "jammed" for about two hours. We were both woozy from beer and "cachaça" when Chico suddenly laughed and said 'I've got an inspiration. Let's do a 10 song LP with just US rock n' roll, call it 'Mistakes of Our Youth' and see what happens." He assured me he could get a good studio musicians backup group together in no time at Philips, and said, "Porra, Arretado' you've got to come along and sing with us." I protested saying my "professional experience" was limited to performing with a buddy at my sister's college and on stage a couple of times in Campina Grande and Recife. He said, "Hey I know your voice, it's pretty good, not great, but it's on key, you know the music, have fun with it, so 'nada de protestar!' [No protesting!] You're in! And the DOPS and 'Censura Prévia' will love it – it is sure to better our (and Chico's) relations with ole' U.S.A. And it might sell some records as well!"

"We did the rehearsal and taping all in one long session, seven hours up at Philips in Alto da Boa Vista. The album released in no time, sales mushroomed and Chico scheduled the concert for Paecambu. You know the rest of the story. Only there is more; we're supposed to go downtown to the 'Censura Prévia' office early next week to 'depor' ['testify']. Jaime you've been through that, and I was with Chico last year. But I've been warned it will be different this time."

Jaime said, "That's for damned sure, the part that I've been through it. That was the heart attack scene last year. Hope to hell I never have to do that again. My only advice: stay cool, don't volunteer any information, answer questions directly and truthfully. Personally, I think it's a love-hate thing; they've got to be tickled pink for the U.S. 'connection' – their most popular singer with publicity in the U.S. singing U.S. rock n' roll! As for Chico's latest and what you wrote about them, be careful, be honest, and play that 'U.S. Citizen, Reporter for the 'Times' - 'What's Going on In Brazil' card. As a favor would you please let us know how all this turns out?"

We sat down to dinner, "pato no tucupi" in honor of the Ferreira's origin in Pará State done with other regional specialties and including a wine from Amazon fruits (yikes, that brought back a memory of that other Amazon concoction Cristina Maria had 'gifted' me with a year ago). She smiled across the table when Jaime poured the wine raving about its qualities. And dinner was topped off with that bitter-sweet açaí ice cream. Most of the talk was small talk, what the two boys were doing in school, Cristina Maria's little sister now at Santa Ursula, and Christina Maria now in first year law school at the Federal University in Rio, a "for-sure" career move in Brazil. Jaime quipped she could do good things for the firm, she laughed and said, "I think I better stay clear of that 'commie-pinko' corporation, don't you think Dad?" "Well, you won't be getting into Itamaraty [The Brazilian State Department] and the Foreign Service; that's for sure."

19

THE BEST LAID PLANS

After dinner and delicious demitasse "cafezinho" it was Cristina Maria herself who said to all, "I'd like to take Mike back to the Castelinho for a little while tonight. I'll fill him in on other matters, you know what I mean, and we can see if he likes the latest in MPB. We might even take a walk on the 'calçada' [Ipanema beach sidewalk]. OK? Mike?"

Dona Regina, not one to say too much, at least up to that point, said, "You know what Rio is like these days; keep a close watch. We would not want 'Arretado' here to be assaulted when he's just made the national scene!"

Cristina Maria said, "Excuse me, got to grab a purse, freshen up and we'll be off in a few minutes. Tell Mom and Dad about life in the great American 'sertão' [outback] of Nebraska, that shouldn't take along, just enough time for me to get ready." All laughed, I feigned protest, saying, "Hey! It's the center of the country! Well, maybe not entertainment or Hollywood or New York or Chicago glitz, but you can go in any direction and in a few days be somewhere a lot more exciting. Seriously, corn, cows and tractors, sand hill cranes, we've got it all! And one of the best college football teams in the nation. Nebraska University is highly respected and not a bad place to be. Besides my family is still scattered all over farms across the state with a smattering down in Kansas. I was getting warmed up, like a Rotarian in Omaha, when Cristina Maria popped back into the room, a short skirt, light sweater with a light jacket on top. We were after all in Carioca "winter" and there could be a very cool breeze from the beach in the evening. I had a sweater with me, thinking of such things when I left Dona Júlia's.

As soon as we got out of the elevator in the foray on the ground floor, I turned to a luscious, beautiful Cristina Maria and asked if this little jaunt was safe, remembering macho Brazilian men, particularly engaged men as protective of their "noivas" [fiancées] as they would be of their wives after the wedding. (Of course, this was not the case of the opposite scene when the same protective husbands had no qualms of hanging out, let's say, at Heitor or Maria Aparecida's place for a night of "relax.") She laughed, said, "I assure you, both you and I are safe; I would not have suggested our 'date' (I like that term) otherwise, but let's get settled in the bar where I can tell you the rest of the story. But for now, if it helps, we are no longer 'noivos' [engaged]. 'Andiamos rapaz.' She offered her arm, I took it and felt the warmth of her hand, and off we went.

The walk to the Castelhinho was short, at most 15 minutes, and most of the conversation was Rio – traffic – "Keep your eyes on <u>all</u> the cars, especially at the crossings and street corners, and there are a lot more motor bikes now. No one follows traffic rules, but you knew that!" Maria Cristina giggles. We arrived to the beachfront bar, understated on the outside but facing the one and only Ipanema Beach. Inside Cristina Maria steered us to a booth toward the back. She said, "It's a lot quieter here and we can talk. I ordered a 'choppe' and she had a Tom Collins. When the drinks arrived, we both raised our glasses and toasted the encounter and each other. I said, "You've pretty well got my news from the house this past hour, not too much to add. It's you we have to talk about." She said, "Soon enough, but I need a detailed run-down on what happened with Molly." I proceeded to tell the story such as it was and is, reiterating that she, Cristina Maria, would come in just as I promised, just the link to Chico and Marieta, knowing of the plans from a year ago. And she engaged to Otávio. "So, it's my turn. What happened and what's happening now?"

"Mike, I had an inkling all this might happen, but really was afraid to admit it to myself or anyone else for that matter, including my best girlfriends, and most of all to Mom and Dad. I didn't lie to you last year when I said I loved Otávio, thought he loved me, and that it wasn't a 'fixed' marriage even though the 'sweetener' might have been Dad's offer to join the company. Still, something did not seem right between us, a 'não sei quê' ['I don't know what'] feeling or vibe. It was a terrific match, his father with a huge road building heavy equipment firm, you can imagine how that is with the Generals' Trans Amazon and other infra-structure projects. The question is, why would he want to join Dad's firm? Concrete is the number one ingredient for Itaipu Dam, the Niterói Bridge, most bridges for the roads, so I guess

Otávio saw a future in it all. You know what makes the wheels turn here – a lot of back scratching!

"But there might be, now in retrospect, another factor or two: his father is a few years younger than Dad, very ambitious and still with big plans for the company, and there are two other brothers already in the firm. My Dad, on the contrary, is older, my two younger brothers are years away from any university degrees, and so far, both say they want nothing to do with business or government. So do the math! What none of us knew was that Otávio was in a hurry, wanting to be in on the major decision making and was pushing Dad on major expansion with big loans from the IMF and backed by the generals. He claimed to have all kinds of connections to Delfim Neto the national finance minister. I think it was a classic case of generations when you get right down to it. Anyway, it did not take long; he and Dad really clashed and one day had the 'big' talk resulting in Otávio saying 'Adeus Jaime, you really missed the boat on this one.'"

I had to interrupt – "Certo. Certo. But where does that leave you? And Otávio?" Cristina Maria quickly answered, "I was getting to that. First of all, it would have been completely impossible for him to 'break' with Dad and the company and stay engaged to me. Things just don't work that way in Brazil, and for that matter, I don't think anywhere. After the blowup with Dad he didn't even have the courtesy to come over or even arrange a meeting with me. He had sworn to Dad he would never step foot in our house again. It was a full week later, this after I kept calling him every day, and no answer, no answer, he finally did call, ask for me, and we arranged a date for dinner and talk.

"He picked the place (as usual, the man does all this in Brazil), that Italian restaurant on the Beach in Posto 6 in Copacabana. We had drinks, an Italian wine he imports just for his family, and he managed the entire six course dinner. I had no appetite at all, nibbled at the food and waited, just waited, for him to finally finish a glass of 'grapa,' have a 'cafezinho' and then look at me. There was sorrow in his eyes, maybe even a tear, but he always was good at having the right show of emotion. I thought it's surely a damned public place to end an engagement. Not my choice. Somehow, I don't know how, we managed to have a civil conversation. The gist of it all was what you already know – he could not continue any relationship with me after leaving the company. 'How in the hell would that work?' I had to agree with him, I think I was in shock, it all seemed to not be happening and I was in a daze. All I remember is taking the engagement ring off my finger, handing to him (over his protest), saying, 'Do me the courtesy of calling me a taxi.' I was in tears by this time, but Mike, really, there was nowhere to go, no direction for us. He said, 'Cristina Maria. I did love you. I guess I loved my job and future more. I'm sorry it all worked out this way. I'm sure it's for the best. You'll understand why I won't be calling. This can't be fixed." He stood up, lightly kissed me on the cheek and went to the maître d and called the cab.

Mom and Dad were at the door when I came in. Both hugged me and tried to express their own sorrow and disappointment. I was too upset to listen, but said, "We can talk about this soon, I'm not sure when. But Dad, I am convinced you were right in what you did. It's pretty clear Otávio's ambition and lust for big things in the business world meant more to him than I did. I' m glad we found out now rather than a year or two from now, maybe after an expensive socialite wedding, a lot of your money down the drain, maybe even a child on the way. Let's talk in the morning or in a day or two.

"What happened was that I made a lot of decisions. First was a trip with girl friends to Spain and France with a lot of wine and moral support. Then, a decision to come back to Rio, get an apartment, study for the Law School exam at the Federal University of Rio de Janeiro and get on with my life. Mike, you don't get jilted like this and not be wounded and scarred. I'm now in first year Law, doing well, seeing no one." She had a serious committed look in her eyes when she said this, but then, suddenly, broke down, sobbing with her head on my shoulder. "Mike, I'm sorry. I'm sorry."

After a while I wiped her tears with a napkin, kissed her gently on the lips, and we both found ourselves repeating a scene from months past. The kiss lasted longer, became passionate. "Cristina Maria, this is a bit insane, on both our parts. There's too much water under the bridge and complications in both our lives to 'go home again.' Let's just hold each other for now. I can be here for you at least for that." She said, "I don't agree. We are both wounded, and I see one wonderful remedy for that. Call a cab, I'll call Mom and Dad and say I'll call them all tomorrow. They knew I would be going to my own apartment tonight anyway. I'm inviting you to take me home, comfort me and you, just for tonight. No strings attached. No tomorrows."

20

THE COMFORT ZONE

Cristina Maria's apartment was small, a two bedroom, but extremely nice and well decorated. After all, her Dad was only too glad to see she had the best, still blaming himself for what had happened, this in spite of her protests. It was not that far from the Castelinho, just a block or two off the commercial business of Conde de Pirauá Street and almost to the canal separating Ipanema from Leblon, almost to the Lagoa Rodrigo de Freitas. We were both a little hesitant or maybe cautious. "A penny for your thoughts," Cristina Maria said to me, "Let me get us a glass of wine and you can tell me about it." I said, "I can't help it. I'm thinking back to my last conversation with Molly, her anger when I said, innocently, that I would probably be seeing you again. It was innocent and honest, and there was no intention on my part of any intimate time or sex with you. Just the situation with Chico and Marieta and you instrumental in all that. There is still some chance, small as it may be, that we will rekindle the relationship. Cristina, I'm incapable of lying, to her, to you, to anyone. It's that damned Catholic upbringing. If we go ahead and relive past times, I'll have to deal with that. The problem is, I'm still at least half in love with you. You are beautiful, intelligent, a really classy Brazilian young lady. I've got all those memories from last year, and besides, it's totally unfair to you with all that has happened and that you only ask moments of comfort, for you and me."

"Miguel, I'm the one who has been unfair. My hurt feelings and tears an hour ago were real, but I would be the last person to endanger your future. On the other hand, we women understand each other a lot better than you men do, no offense intended. You are not the one who cut off the relationship. You're not to blame.

You are being too hard on yourself. It isn't like we are starting a love affair. We are two hurt human beings and there is nothing wrong, pardon my disdain for all that 'merda' of sin the Church and its clergy preach, nothing wrong with this moment." She was holding my hand in hers and leaned forward and gave me a warm kiss.

It was then that emotions ruled, hormones, whatever you want to call it. I said, "You've convinced me; we both understand each other." I kissed her again, this time more deeply, and began to pull up her sweater and loosen the belt to her skirt. She said, "There's a better way to do this. Let's relive some history and good times. I still have the Amazon 'miracle,' you still have not lost your zest, so let's have more wine, refresh ourselves in my shower and see what happens!" She took my hand, led me to the shower and we both slowly undressed each other, taking our time and sipping now from a bottle of champagne she pulled from the refrigerator.

"Meu Deus, you are one sexy lady." I was already aroused at the thought of it all. Cristina laughed, said, "You are right about that. It's been such a long time, I was 'saving myself' for the wedding night. That was pretty stupid, huh?"

I'll not go on with all the details, somewhat of a replay from a year ago and in "Letters II", suffice to say we both meshed well, first in caresses in the shower and then in bed. We made passionate love, not talking much until collapsing together in bed and cooling off with no sheets on. After a while Cristina Maria jumped out of bed, bounded off to the bathroom and came back waving that small familiar bottle from last time. Laughing and tickling me, she rubbed it liberally on my penis, on her breasts and vagina, capped the bottle saying, "Can't have that spill!" filled our glasses and climbed into bed again. The stuff worked and a few minutes later we were close to exhaustion. I wanted to say something, but she put her finger up to my lips, said, "Maybe in the morning. Remember all this is to comfort us if just for a night."

She was up before I was in the morning, dressed in a very sexy blue negligee, and had steamy "café com leite" and croissants ready. Propped up on pillows we had what would be our last talk. I said, "Nothing's changed but everything has changed. I'm available, you're available, but for what? I haven't even considered the possibility of reconsidering life in Brazil, didn't know there was even a chance. You seem to be on track to getting along with your life. Nossa! Where does that leave us?"

Cristina said, "Bobo ["dummy"], just where I said yesterday. We comforted each other. I think you could say we succeeded on that account. I know I feel better. I think you would be better off thinking what you are going to say to General Goeldi downtown next week. I've got an uneasy feeling this time about all this. I'll tell you,

I've got some contacts at the Law School, on the 'right' side with the government, and if you need a lawyer that the generals will talk to, they can arrange it. Why don't you give me a call when you know more? "She kissed me slightly on the lips, helped me get dressed, gave me a tight hug and deeper kiss and said, "Miguel, I'll treasure our times."

Like before, this was another chapter of our relationship, but not for "Letters."

21

MAKING PLANS FOR THE CENSORSHIP BOARD

As planned, or not, Chico called me at Dona Júlia's house the next Monday: "Oi Arretado, nós temos um compromisso com General Goeldi amanhã às 10 horas. ["Hey, Cool Guy, we have an appointment with General Goeldi in the morning at 10:00."] Why don't you take a taxi to my house at 8:00, we'll work out some strategy. Não se preocupe – I told you I'd take care of you. And I've got some wild news and an idea or two. See you then?" I said fine I'd be there. I'm apprehensive especially after talking to Heitor Dias, but if anyone knows his way around the "Censura" office it's Chico.

Tuesday rolled around, all too quickly with a lack of sleep on my part. I ate Dona Júlia's quick "café com leite" and sweet rolls and grabbed a taxi to Chico's house. Marieta was there with him in the living room, steaming cafezinhos and "pão doce" [sweet rolls] to the side. She smiled and then laughed, "Miguel I had no idea. That alcohol toot ['porre'] you and Chico put on the other day turned into all this! Meu Deus! Quem me dera haver adivinhado," ["Who could have guessed"]. Chico cut in, saying, "Marieta, Miguel and I have to talk strategy and we've only got about an hour. You can join in, you've got really good ideas sometimes, or not. I'm going to fill him in on the latest, work out a plan for General Goeldi and then be downtown by 10:00, not much time. The general does not like to be kept waiting."

He turned to me. "Miguel, I've got word through a source (I'm got friends in high places, I'm not supposed to know these things), that ole' Goeldi may lower the boom on both you and me, cancelling all my future shows and ushering you out of the country, pronto! Marieta and I, frankly, need the money from the concerts, too many bills to pay here with the house and car and kids. But I think I can 'driblar' ['fool'] his plan and maybe do something surprising to make him change his mind. I've been thinking about this ever since Paecambu. A question, that visa I arranged for you is for a year, right? I'm not thinking a year, but a month or two might be important.

"Here's my angle for the 'censura:' as per custom, we are gracious and hear first of all everything he has to say, I'm guessing the 'cease and desist' order. Then I'll say, all surprised and agog, 'General I've got a plan that I think is good for all of us.' I'll offer to do a series of concerts at all the big 'faraônico' [Pharaoh - like projects] - here in Rio at the Monument to the Soldiers of World War II, the 'Big Double I' down at Glória; then the new Rio – Niterói bridge along the new 'autopista' [freeway] out to the Galeão Airport, and then out to Itaipu Dam, and maybe João Pessoa at the entrance to the Amazon Highway. But here's the kicker: we'll call the tour "Mistakes from Our Youth, Better Times Ahead, Por Enquanto" ["For Now"], indirectly letting the brass know all I've done lately is a mistake, do all ten rock n' roll songs and then ten old harmless sambas from 1965, 1966, and 1967 before all the 'merda' hit the fan. 'Arretado,' I've got it from all kinds of sources, my music producer at Philips, public relations and advance men from my concerts, that there is a large contingent of Brazilians who will not only like this, but 'get' the sub-text, i.e. the Brazil of the generals is what it is, these projects are for the good of Brazil, let's relax, have some fun and live the moment. What is not being said will be the most important, 'por enquanto!'

"The only fly in the ointment is the Left, and there are a lot of them. They will at first crucify me for having sold out, there will be a few 'vaias' ['boos'] at the concerts, but I'm betting and gambling that most fans will enjoy the moment. We will salt the main program in Portuguese with references to the "Cordel," the plight of the northeasterner workers, and how the government projects will at least bring some jobs. You can take ten minutes, explain the 'Cordel' stories of the 'retirantes,' [migrants] and I'll sing 'Pedro Pedreiro.' I guarantee there will be applause. But I've got to have you to carry it off. How about it?

"Arretado,' we've got twenty minutes in the taxi for you to make up your mind. Otherwise, it's Senhor Goeldi's solution. Get your stuff together, we've got to get going downtown. Don't say anything, just let him talk and I'll take over after that. And by the way, I'll arrange a one-year performing "union card" for you (required of all musicians here, like your Ascap union card in the States), expenses will be taken care of (we eat, drink and live well) and there'll be a nice 'honorarium' to buy you a top of the line, real Brazilian rosewood classic guitar when we're done! Or you can just spend it all on 'choppe,' 'cachaça' and Brazilian women!"

I wasn't expecting any of the above and stuttered a nearly incoherent reply, "Okay, we'll see, but I've got classes in Lincoln in a couple of weeks and don't see how this can fit. And besides, once again, I'm not a professional musician." Chico said, "There you are wrong – the recording and Paecambu was your baptism of fire and you passed the test. You can always get a temporary leave of absence, não é? [right?]" There was time for nothing else. The taxi took us through Jardim Botânico, Laranjeiras, the back of Botafogo, down to the Aterro and on downtown. Chico bounded out of the taxi, slapped me on the shoulder and said, "Remember my instructions. 'Bora, rapaz, lembre 'O Brasil pra' frente,' ["Let's go, guy; remember "Onward and Upward Brazil"] and he winked at me as we walked up the steps to the Censorhip building.

22

AN INVITATION TO LEAVE, BUT WAIT!

There was actually an armed guard outside the main office, but when he saw Chico he smiled and said, "Bom Dia, de novo aqui seu' Chico? They are waiting on you and your friend. Go on inside and have a seat." "They?" Chico said. The guard said, "Calma. Just be patient. You'll know soon enough."

We walked in and were greeted right away by the tall, distinguished gentleman I remembered as General Goeldi. He reintroduced himself and said simply, "This is Coronel Lopes, he is my assistant here at "Censura Prévia" [CP] and has full access to any current business or affairs. Please take a seat; there are several matters to discuss and I'm afraid with somewhat limited time.

"Chico, if you don't mind, I'll address the issues with our good friend Michael first and get to the more serious issues later. Mike, first of all, welcome back to Brazil; I'm glad we have a chance to meet again. Your 'Letters' of last year reflected very correctly and positively on our first meeting here with Chico in this office. Well and good. Your new endeavor as 'parceiro' ['partner'] and entertainer with Chico on 'Mistakes of Our Youth' I must admit is quite a turn of events. We of course kept track of the evolution of it all, including the recording session and the considerable success in the market! Nosso Senhor! It was not only a surprise but a pleasure to see old friend Chico, veteran of a lot of scrapes with us, joining you in Rock n' Roll in English. I think it was indeed good for Brazil – U.S. Relations to see how friendships and culture could mix successfully in the Brazilian entertainment scene. So far so good. The 'Mistakes' sector of the concert at Paecambu also was a happy moment and demonstrated what good things can be done if one has the right mindset and good intentions. Congratulations to both of you.

"However," and now the General sat down at his desk, lit a Marlboro (ha!) and toyed with the cigarette and ashtray, turned much more serious and continued. "Miguel, there is a much more serious matter; it's related to 'Construção' and 'Deus Lhe Pague.' You wrote in your last 'Letter' to the NYT quoting verses from both songs, but much beyond that, and worse according to our perspective, explaining the entire songs and their 'social' meaning and context. I'm afraid that was when you crossed the line. The gist of that 'Letter' indeed did not put Brazil and especially our government in a good light. I've talked it over with the people at Itamaraty: we are prepared to revoke your visa and escort you to Galeão Airport and the flight of your choice, but <u>out</u> of Brazil. We don't need to review our entire file on you, but let's just say this is the 'last straw.' Your initial friendship with Colonel Cavalcanti Proença, invited to "retire" as a line officer and become a professor of Literature at our "West Point," research on the communist novelist Jorge Amado, your friendship with Ariano Suassuna who has also criticized the government, and hanging out with the wrong people in Recife and even here in Rio color your past. Particularly bothersome is your connection to the Jaime Ferreira family. And incidentally, I think you have forgotten the transportation of a firearm from Juazeiro to a leftist student in Recife in 1966, although we know you were naïve in much of the matter. That was a capital offense you wiggled out of. But you still did it. So we come to the present; we believe the last 'Letter' confirms our suspicions of your sympathy to the Left. I admit it's not all cut and dried; you are a good American and patriot, but the matter is delicate, and we can't have any further 'mistakes' pardon the cross-reference to Chico's latest album."

Chico started to talk, but I waved an arm at him and stammered a response, "General, if I may just say in my own defense, I am totally pro-democracy, that is what my country and all its beliefs are based on. It's not so much that I am against the Military Revolution of 1964; I'm as anti-communist as anyone and afraid of both Fidel Castro and Ché Guevara and what they might accomplish in Latin America. I was a huge fan of President John F. Kennedy and the Alliance for Progress and even volunteered to work with Bobby Kennedy before his assassination. My original research grant here two years ago was a small part of a primary effort by the U.S. government to fight the spread of Russian Communism. I'm totally against leftist violence in Brazil, the kidnappings, the bank robberies, the bombing and attempted assassination of General Costa e Silva in Recife in 1966. (You might remember I reported on it in 'Letters I.') But what I cannot countenance is your government's own reaction of press censorship, restricting the right of free speech and association. I interpreted Chico's music as his right to comment on Brazil and life here at present."

"Thank you. Mike you are very naïve. Your heart is in the right place, but you are blindfolded to the harm your last 'Letter' did to us. Our decision stands."

I think I must have turned two shades of pale by then, my inner self wanting to rebut the General, but common sense (and all the advice from Chico and others) telling me to keep my mouth shut. I had already said too much. Breathing a bit quicker, sweating some, maybe just what the CP wanted, I was about to issue a protest, weak as it might be, when Chico raised his hand (like in grade school) and said, "General I think I can help in this matter and clarify some things perhaps at the same time but not making excuses for Mike." General Goeldi, still in stern all-business mode, said, "Go ahead Chico, but make it quick. Our time is limited."

"First of all, and with all due respect, whatever Mike wrote in his 'Letters' was a result of my explanation of the two songs. 'Certo,' they commented metaphorically on life in today's Brazil, the life of the construction worker is exactly what I described in the song. As for 'Deus Lhe Pague' I admit it is much darker and shows the demeanor of the more general populace. Maybe I did go a bit overboard in that, but it has nothing to do with Mike. He reported what I explained to him. But General, I've had a brainstorm that I think may be good for all of us, especially you in the government and the current situation. Can I take ten minutes and explain it?"

"Chico, it better be good. Ten minutes. That's all."

Chico then proceeded to tell the general what I have already mentioned, the "patriotic" concerts at the government's huge economic projects, doing a repeat of "Mistakes of Our Youth" but adding a cultural section on "Cordel," the northeastern migrants' story by me, and (at my suggestion) singing "Asa Branca" (the "Northeastern Anthem" by Luís Gonzaga of "Forró" music fame), "Pedro Pedreiro" (Chico's version of the same) and a set of non-political samba like "A Banda" and others from his earlier phase of recording. He added that he would be doing so at some risk, meaning those who will say he is "selling out to the regime," but that there is demand and support among Brazilians for such a concert. He added "It's an olive branch of peace and support of the Government Projects because I do believe they will add jobs for many of the populace. And besides, General, Marieta and I need the money. We would start at the Soldiers' Memorial in Glória, at the Rio - Niteroi Bridge, on the dam construction site at Itaipu, and finally at the beginning of the Transamazon Highway in João Pessoa. But in return, the concert would carry the label at its end of advertising, 'Por Enquanto' ["For the time being"]. That's fair enough I think, tit for tat. What do you say?"

General Goeldi said, "Chico I think this is very generous of you and Michael (in a minor role), but I've got to toss it around with some of my colleagues on the War Staff. It's an offer that bears consideration. I think I can let you know in two days. But a warning, if it brings massive protests, I will shut it down, and in a hurry. Fair enough? That will be all for today; you'll be hearing from me in two days." He shook hands with both of us, and basically said "Adeus, and like you say, 'Por Enquanto.' It works both ways."

Chico was guarded in the taxi on the way home saying he would prefer to talk about it at home but thought that things looked somewhat positive. He said, "Miguel, I've never risked my career before like this, but porra! It may be the right thing for right now." At home he got out the Pitú bottle, opened some Brahma Choppe for me, sat back on the divan, took a deep breath, sighed and said, "It's all in the labeling. I'm thinking of the 'manchete' [headline] for the concerts – 'What's Good for Brazil – the Promise of Jobs – a Tribute to the Past and Hope for the Future. Por Enquanto.' Educated Brazilians, those that know any history and even doubters around 'Brasil 'pra frente' will support it. But it's risky, very risky, lots to think about and plan."

The next day General Goeldi called Chico and said, "Good news. My colleagues on the War Staff have approved the idea – 4 concerts – the War Memorial in Rio, the Rio-Niteroi Bridge, Itaipu, and the Transamazonic start in João Pessoa. The program you suggested: 'Mistakes from Our Youth,' Northeastern homage with 'Asa Branca' and 'Pedro Pedreiro,' and 'old' samba. You must submit a song list before final approval. There will be a government presence at each concert, and project financiers and labor representatives. I'm sure TV Globo and others will film and report the concerts as 'news' as well. Please send the song list." Chico after some thought sent the following list:

"A Banda," "Amanhã Ninguém Sabe," "Você Não Ouviu," "Olé – Olá,"

"A Rita," "Meu Refrão," "Madalena Foi P'ro Mar," "Tem Mais Samba," "Juca," and "Valsinha,"

Chico said, "I'm sure this will please the old-timers, nostalgia folks, but not in the least any of the protesters of today. We're taking a big chance here."

23

WHAT'S WORLD WAR II GOT TO DO WITH IT?

The concerts were scheduled for the next four weeks. Advanced publicity came with Chico's "manchete" [headline] adding the now premise of "Por Enquanto" at the end. "O Globo" in Rio and "A Folha de São Paulo" immediately wrote front page articles on the concert tour, and news coverage soon followed by "Globo TV" and the national media. Response from the Left was immediate, boycott the concerts! That was fine with Chico, the generals, and the minor figure, me. Better than planned demonstrations, but not to be ruled out. We rehearsed at Chico's house and he prepped us on all possibilities, particularly me, the newcomer. "O' gente! ["Oxente" in Northeastern parlance. "My My"].

THE WORLD WAR II SOLDIERS' MEMORIAL AND GLÓRIA DISTRICT

One week later the big experiment rolled into action. The first concert was that Monday at the World War II Memorial in Glória District with the Bay of Guanabara in the background. It is an iconic scene in Rio – the huge concrete monument in the form of a gigantic dual columned I with a platform on top, the figures of soldiers of the different armed forces to the side. The monument and museum were completed in 1960. There was a large space around both for the anticipated crowd. No one could have figured on the outcome – thousands of fans, many of the "velha guarda" or old generation included, waving the blue, green, and yellow Brazilian flag, shouting and singing Chico's songs. Few Brazilians really knew the story of Brazil's limited participation in World War II, but that rather than the dictatorship (for the most part) was in the national mindset for the monument. I think it was Chico's speech before the concert that swung the atmosphere and response in our favor. Basically it reiterated the themes of the "manchete" [headline] in Chico's words (which I paraphrase from the moment):

"Povo brasileiro! Obrigado por chegar hoje ao nosso concerto e este momento. ["Thanks for coming to our concert today and this moment."] Once again recall our theme, 'What's Good for Brazil – A Tribute to the Past – Jobs and Hope for the Future – 'Por Enquanto'. The program for today is just that: songs of the 1950s and my and perhaps your nostalgia for our crazy teen years – thus 'Mistakes from Our Youth'" – Rock n' Roll with the help of my good friend 'Arretado,' homage to our northeastern migrants and workers, the hope for new jobs for them and all Brazilians, and happier days with MPB and our early 'sambas.' Enjoy." There was delirious applause along with a few boos.

We launched into the same rock n' roll from Paecambu, the crowd on their feet and dancing. Then Chico introduced me, more applause but less subdued and an occasional "Yankee go home," until I gave a five minute introduction to the importance of "A Literatura de Cordel," the story of the migrants from the Northeast, their contribution as workers in Rio, São Paulo and Brasília, and introduced our homage with "Asa Branca" and Chico's "Pedro Penseiro." The crowd was on its feet and most sang along to both pieces. No one could argue with either. It was hard to tell, but I think I saw many hundreds of Northeasterners in the crowd. Then Chico and band (minus me on stage but now in the front row of the audience) launched into the old "sambas." Applause and cheering brought an uproar, especially with "A Banda." All were shouting afterwards, "Bis. Bis" ["Again. Again"]. So they played "A Banda" again and Chico repeated "Meu Refrão" ["My Refrain"] most in the audience understanding it was his way of maintaining dignity and his stance in Brazil, but in a friendly way prior to censorship. The audience got the message. And the generals could not argue. The lyrics won him the day:

> Quem Canta Comigo Canta Meu Refrão
> He who sings with me sings my refrain
> Meu melhor amigo é meu violão.
> My best friend is my guitar.
> The verse:
> O refrão que eu faço é p'ra você saber
> The refrain that I do is for you to know
> Que eu não vou dar braço p'ra ninguém torcer.
> I'm not going to offer my arm for anyone to twist.

"Obrigado mais uma vez. Vamos ter esperança para o futuro. Por enquanto! Veremos todos na Ponte Rio-Niterói a semana que vem!" ["Thanks again. Let's have hope for the future. For now! We'll see all of you at the Rio-Niterói Bridge next week."]

After wading through a crowd of well-wishers, Chico giving many autographs and even yours truly one or two, we loaded all the equipment into a big van and headed for Chico's house. There was much laughter, many "abraços" [embraces] amidst the "Brahma Choppe" and "Pitu." Chico was all smiles saying it had gone really well, no big protests (a sigh of relief), and what seemed like real enthusiasm from the crowd. As we all partied a bit, the phone was ringing off the hook the whole time. General Goeldi interrupted Chico's talk and the celebration calling and pronouncing it a success. Chico said, "Nossa! Even Luís Gonzaga called thanking me and us for it all, and also for the plug for 'Asa Branca'! And Philips just called and said the old LP with 'Pedro Pedreiro' has a new life! So 'p'ra frente Brasil,' and we'll meet here early Friday for rehearsal and then all head up to the bridge on Monday. If Rio-Niteroi Ponte bureaucrats get their act together, we'll be in the middle of the bridge and have an hour and one-half for the concert. No danger other than Frigate Bird poop on our heads. And maybe static from the wind (José our sound guy says he can fix that). The bridge will be closed to traffic, allowing the crowd in at noon, another hour to clear out after the concert and open again at 3:00. No one is complaining, it's one of the few things the government has done to make that commute from hell from Rio to Niterói and back a better thing. Personally, I like the ferry boats, but then again I don't live on one side and work on the other. Tá combinado? Até a sexta-feira" ["It's all set. See you on Friday."].

Chico cornered me on the way out, saying he did not want to talk in front of the others, "Arretado, you did great! You're getting used to the stage and I think even your guitar was in tune. The northeastern set was a huge success. But you should know there were a few phone calls to Philips to get rid of the 'gringo.' I don't think you are in danger, after all, the 'macacos' ['gorillas'] have to protect us all, but if you want to bail out, I can do the intro to 'Asa Branca' and 'Pedro Pedreiro.' What do you think?"

"Chico, I've already got a leave of absence from the U. of Nebraska and I'm having the time of my life. Why stop now? If you keep your promise, maybe now I can afford a Giannini rosewood instead of the Di Giorgio. All this is surreal, but I'm ready to keep living the dream. I think I'll go back to the library at the 'Casa de Rui' tomorrow, see what else I can dig up on the Northeasterners in Rio, maybe even construction work on the bridge. Plan on me here for the rehearsal on Friday and up on the bridge Monday."

He gave me one of those big 'carioca' embraces, smiled and said, "Arretado, life is short, we're doing the right thing. These moments will not come again, just a quirk in Brazilian living! I'm happy you're coming along. Chau. Até a sexta. [See you on Friday]. Don't be surprised if you have to sign some autographs on the street; this was all televised by TV Rede Globo so you are a 'marked man,' but hey, in the good sense."

24

THE OTHON AND A WARNING

Nothing had changed in my routine, taking the "slow bus" through Copacabana, through the tunnels and along the beach in Botafogo, then the twenty-minute walk up to the Casa de Rui on São Clemente street. There were some unexpected stops, mainly from smiling 'carioca' girls but even guys, saying "Parabens" ["congratulations"] and asking for autographs. I had to learn to remember to keep my BIC pens in my briefcase.

There was a bit of a dither at the Casa Research Center, embraces from the old-time research center staff along with "Arretado, welcome home. Back to 'Cordel' research is it?" After regaling them with some not too exaggerated stories of the concert, I was on my way to the library when old friend Felipe from the Philology Section sidled up and said, "Hey, I wasn't wrong was I? Are you exhausted yet?" He's the one who told me one time I should be exhausted from adventures in Rio, meaning, screwing the carioca chicks. I smiled and went on to the library, and one change, no longer did they have to get my list of requests for the story-poems, find them and deliver them to the research desk, but let me go directly to the stacks. One benefit of notoriety.

Another came along as I was digging through the old file boxes that held the story-poems. A familiar face turned up next to me; I remembered her from the Congress party when she had said, "My turn next time." Who can forget? It was Sônia. She smiled and wondered if there was anything she could help me with, rubbing a svelte but stacked body next to mine. Whoa! I thought, "Where's Claudia?" She laughed and said she was off today but maybe we could work something out, sooner rather than later. She said, "If you are amenable, I'll meet you in the rooftop bar on top of the Othon Hotel at 7:00 o'clock and I'll have a room for the two of us. Daddy gets coupons from them and gives me one once in a while for a treat, but he doesn't say who my roommates have to be." Giggle. "I know you like to have fun, so why not?" I found myself a bit stunned, temporarily forgetting about story-poems on the bridge construction, thought "So, what harm can it do?" and said that would be fine with me. She planted a big kiss on my lips, swung her hips around and disappeared around the corner. Whew, I thought, I had an inkling this might happen sometime, but you can't guess when. In all honesty it had been a while, still remembering Cristina Maria, but no harm done. The reader is wondering when I'm going to get back to serious research and down to work. I tried. History repeated itself.

I was seated at one of the research desks and ole' Heitor Dias walked in. "Oi Arretado! Let's talk; we can go outside to the garden here in front." I left all my stuff, briefcase, pens and notes on the desk and followed him out. It was another one of those invitations I could not refuse, i.e. a DOPS invitation. He asked me to join him on one of the benches facing all the palm trees and tropical plants, lit up a Marlboro and said,

"I've got to admit you are the most interesting person I've had orders to keep track of here in Rio. Meu Deus, this is all like a TV soap opera. I think Claudia was the last featured heroine since we've talked. Oh yeah, I forgot Maria Aparecida. She says hi by the way and is a bit miffed you haven't been by. But your one-nighter with Cristina Maria wasn't bad for 'sobremesa' ['dessert']. Ha ha. Don't get insulted, just part of the job. I wasn't in São Paulo at Paecambu but my buddies who were filled me in, and of course there was word from General Goeldi's office and that 'interview.' Porra! Then the damned War Memorial Concert. I don't know many big words, but I guess that's Chico's 'détente' with the government. I was in the crowd and expecting the worst because we had it there would be a protest from the commie left and maybe even a Molotov cocktail or two. You lucked out my friend. It turns out we still have some patriots here in Brazil, especially a lot of the old timers at the concert. And we're gearing up to keep you company on the Rio-Niteroi bridge next week.

"But I'm happy to see you haven't forgotten your so-called 'work' and are back here at your old 'ponto' ['hangout']. Maybe I was wrong about the northeastern 'cabeça-chatas' ['flat heads'] swarming around Rio. Luís Gonzaga's 'forró' shit is all over the airwaves and 'Asa Branca' is damned near a northeastern anthem. I listened to it and admit it almost made <u>me</u> cry; I wish they would have all got on that train Chico sings about and quit contaminating Rio.

"Anyway, back down to business. There are a lot of us at DOPS that think this merry go around is due to come off the hinges. The commie-perverts on the Left are a lot fewer, but a lot more desperate. And they don't like Chico's turn to 'cooperation' with the regime worth a damn. You won't see us, but we are doubling our presence for next week at the bridge. If anything happens, all hell will break loose. A lot of unhappy and bunged up people both from the right and left. A lot of people will get hurt. But personally, you are my ole' buddy now and I wouldn't want anything to happen to you. I have some free advice, jump off this train and just do your library work like a good egghead professor. No one will think the less of you for it. You've had your fun. How about it?"

"My turn Heitor. I think you've coming around it bit, I mean about the northeasterners. There will be some jobs for them, I don't know how many, but at least some with the big projects; that's why Chico is doing all this. I'm just going along for the ride. He and Marieta however are hoping for a much-needed paycheck. I appreciate your concern for my safety, maybe you can get some big guys to get me out of there next week if you're right. I don't think it will happen. Let's give it another try, porra! This might be a good turn from Chico's 'Roda Viva' ['Ferris Wheel'] song and metaphor about life under the regime and the concert you closed down a while back in Porto Alegre (the DOPS closed down the concert for being 'antithetical' to the regime). A happier time and place. Pardon my metaphor, but a new go-round and turn of events. Anyway, the concert's scheduled and it may just be another feather in his cap for General Goeldi and company."

"So be it, 'Arretado,' but don't say I didn't warn you. We can hope for the best. Changing the subject, what's next on your fun list? Who is it this time? I guess you and we will know soon enough. I wish I could tag along. We'll be in touch after the concert, and I hope no one will have any broken bones."

Heitor snubbed out his second cigarette, gave me the 'carioca' embrace and said "Até já Arretado. ["See you, Arretado."] Don't make waves. And don't fall off the bridge."

25

THE PENTHOUSE SUITE. RODRIGUES LMTD. A PROPOSAL

I have to admit some mixed emotions, but damn who has time for politics when the Othon and Sonia were waiting. I left the Center with a lot of "abraços" and "boa sorte" ["good luck"] for the next week, caught a decrepit São Clemente bus to Botafogo beach, transferred to a Copa bus and soon was back at Dona Júlia's. She wanted to talk, have another Pitú and get the news. I told her I had a big date that night and had to clean up. She smiled that Cearense smile and said, "You know you've got a private room here; we can keep a secret, bring her on over. I'll even provide the champagne." I impulsively gave her a kiss on the cheek and a light embrace and said, "Not yet Dona Júlia, but who knows? Have you wired my room yet?" She laughed, I cleaned up, and it was just a short walk to the beach and the Othon.

COPACABANA BEACH FROM THE OTHON

I took the elevator up to the terrace – bar – night club up on top. This was the place I discovered as a poor student back in 1967 when capitalism had not caught up with Brazil – a small bottle of Brahma Choppe beer for 25 cents U.S.D. The next time in 1969 it was three dollars! The place hadn't changed much, bar stools up front with the best view I had ever seen of Copacabana beach, a step down to tables and chairs for the drink and dancing crowd. A trio was already playing in the background, music to my taste, smooth, quiet Bossa Nova, probably the only place in all Rio de Janeiro where you didn't need ear plugs to quiet the din. I heard a "psst," that Brazilian way of getting your attention, and there she was in all her glory seated at one of the tables, Sonia off-duty from the stacks at the Casa de Rui.

"Oi Arretado! Let's have a couple of 'caipirinhas' here before the main course! I thought this view, the music and hey, me, would agree with you. I think I know enough about you, Claudia can't keep a secret, but you may want to know a little about me. She waved the waiter over, ordered the drinks, and without any comment from me other than a "go ahead," told me her "story," another lesson in life in Brazil for this gringo.

"Just like most of us at the Casa de Rui, the job is a bit onerous, lousy pay, but it is in effect an internship at a prestigious place until something else comes along. And it will. I've got an undergraduate friggin' degree in Library Science, thus the connection to the Casa, but a Law degree as well. That makes me one of the tens of thousands unemployed lawyers in Rio! Ha ha. Fortunately, in my case there's no hurry.

"By the way, the last name is Rodrigues; I doubt if you have heard of the Rodrigues Ltd. firm, but it's huge real estate company here in Rio, all kinds of properties from high rise condos out in the Barra (Rio's newest and most exclusive residential area for the rich wanting to get away from the old 'squalor' of Copacabana, Ipanema and Leblon). Ha ha again. But as well a big hunk of commercial properties all over the city, downtown, new high rises near the Fort in Copacabana, and the beach community south all the way to Barra. Daddy runs the whole shebang, keeps me in allowance money, (ha ha again), but insists the Casa de Rui with its prestige is a good first step, in what I don't know. Getting to know how the 'other half,' the struggling middle class and intellectuals live. Ha ha.

"I'm sure after my 'training' he'll have a nice cozy office for me. Have you been to that gated living - office building near the Fort? We own that. I know I'm coming on pretty strong with all this, dealing with a professor from the U.S. and a folklorist, 'cordel' specialist at that, but no reason you can't experience 'uma filha de ricaços' [a rich man's daughter] in your sojourn in 'the marvelous city.' But I'm not stupid and am well aware of what's going on in Brazil. I've spent many vacations in the Northeast and saw a lot more than the beaches. That doesn't make me a convert to the Left, one of the nasty 'commie-perverts' my dad hates, but believe me I am pretty well informed. I read lots of our literature including the 'Novelists of the Northeast,' Graciliano, Raquel, Zé Lins and Jorge Amado, so I'm aware of the old oligarchy on the plantations and the class struggle, but more of damned good literature. I know of your connection to Ariano Suassuna, one of my favorites, so we do have something in common. Like everyone else in the upper class in Rio, Chico Buarque is an obsession and a great pleasure in my life. My 'invitation' today goes a little beyond that. Your connection and all that's happened the last two weeks with Chico and his band is a surprise and revelation. So maybe you can include me in a little of your adventure, at least for tonight."

"Sonia, thanks. That's a mouthful, kind of makes me wonder where my sentiments are, overall in Brazil, and me dealing with it. I've always had a few upper-class connections here, one from the very beginning going back to Jesuit undergraduate days at Georgetown, and a couple more in Recife and Rio. I'm not a Communist either, but I believe in democracy and think Brazil can do a lot better for the underprivileged. Dom Hêlder Câmara in Recife is one of the persons I believe has his priorities in order. And yeah, I know your building, an unexpected connection to Gisele Fernandes and 'O Globo.' One of her 'tele-novelas' [soap operas] coming to real life, the murder of her actress-daughter, all reported in the 'Cordel,' took me to her office in what turns out to be your Dad's building for an interview. I have never seen a more beautiful view in Rio than that from her office-studio. My research is literature and 'Cordel,' but if you have read any of the 'Letters' to the 'Times' and the first book from 1969 you'll know I'm to be aware of the full experience in Brazil. And that includes having some fun. My engagement to a wonderful gal in Washington D.C. just broke off before this trip, so I'm 'legal' to come what may. Saúde!" We clicked glasses.

We had a couple of "caipirinhas" and even danced a bit to the Bossa Nova, recalling gringos can't dance samba except maybe after two "caipirinhas." Or is it three? Sônia took charge, took me by the hand and headed to the elevator. Much to my surprise, only one floor down from the top terrace; she unlocked the room door and porra! We were in a luxury suite. Two queen beds, divan, easy chairs, nice paintings on the wall, and an incredible view of most all of Copa beach since this was a corner room with view to the ocean ahead and to the far east end of the crescent of Copacabana with that view of Sugar Loaf in the distance. I was open-mouthed and big eyes with it all. Sônia laughed, saying, "I didn't tell you that Rodrigues Real Estate Limited also has a share in the Othon. I hope you don't mind. This is all on the company! Room service and whatever we want from the frigo bar. Champanha?" She opened a bottle of the same, poured our glasses, gave me a close hug and long kiss and said, "Let's enjoy the view before the main course. Tá?"

The reader my feel like we've been here before, Cristina Maria, Cláudia, Maria Aparecida, Mike Gaherty was enjoying his "off time" from the band. "Viver é muito perigoso. Aproveite!" ["Living is very dangerous. Carpe Diem"). Sônia was a product of her class, blond coifed hair with stylish brown streaks from the weekly salon visit, and that upper class "carioca" clothing, more to be discovered in a moment. She ordered a late evening 'ceia' [dinner] from room service which included small lobsters, a small filet mignon, that good rice with vegetables, and fries, saying, "Don't eat too much; I thought we might need some energy before 'dessert.' And there's more champagne." She laughed and seemed to want to talk more as we enjoyed the entire view while sitting on a divan facing the ocean.

"Mike, tell me about the girl in D.C. We 'cariocas' like to know the competition. Não se preocupe! [Don't worry!] I think you've got some grieving to do and I can help with that. No strings attached, 'por enquanto!' I'm thinking we can become good friends after tonight."

"Sônia, you're making me a bit nervous. I think I still love Molly in D.C., but right now that's on the back burner. She was pretty definitive about the breakup, but hey, I'm going home soon, back to the academic grind in Lincoln with lots of work to do, but a guy can get lonely in Lincoln. I guess you could say that when I got on the airplane for the Congress which seems like a year ago now I made a conscious decision to return to bachelor days and have some fun. I can't tell you, well, you know a lot of it, how amazingly it has turned out. I haven't been lonely here. You however are indeed a pleasant surprise. Big stuff is happening next week, the Rio-Niterói concert, and Itaipu after that, but let's live a little for now."

Sônia smiled, said she agreed, but that there would be plenty of time to talk about more serious matters in the morning. The incredible "lanche" [snack] arrived (that's what she called it), we enjoyed it thoroughly, had more wine, the room service waiters came and cleared all in good order (they seemed to be familiar with how it should all go, all business like and very discreet). No need to go into all the details, but Sônia knew her way around the bedroom. I must say she dazzled in bra and panties and more when she deposited them on the floor for our shower with 'carioca' foreplay which is like what is supposed to go on after foreplay. A wonderful night when all cares were forgotten, and sexual appetites were satiated. What happened after that was the mini "bombshell." Leaning on a pillow she started talking again, but in a serious vein.

"Mike, I hope you won't think me forward, and we hardly know each other. But I know all about you, from all the headache causing research at the Casa, and from talk with all kinds of sources I'd rather not reveal, but you can guess. This may surprise you, in fact, I'm sure it will. Maybe I've a little defensive. I am not a spoiled rich brat; there are literally up to a dozen 'well-bred, rich and influential Daddy's boys' after me. Even your old friend Caetano Forti and his brother have shown their interest, no matter they are both supposedly happily married. No one can see why I'm still at the Casa and 'not doing more with my life.' There is a very good chance I could get engaged, marry one of the suitors and not lift a finger the rest of my life. But the parties, style shows, charity events, salon visits with all the gossip, society page pictures in the best magazines, and even Ivo Pitanguy plastic surgery in my future (you can see I'm not ready for that) have no appeal to me. And I've already seen the world, first class in the company Lear jet, bathed on Miami Beach and rested in our 25th story luxury condo (doesn't everyone have one?) after the shopping and parties with any kind of stimulant you might imagine. I want you to know all this and listen to my 'modest proposal.' It's crazy but it's not pie in the sky.

"Mike, let me propose to you a possibility. My only request is you hear me out and not make fun of what I say. If we were to continue to see each other, if we clicked, the sky is the limit. I will indeed take my place in the Company world; I can easily get or arrange an advanced degree from the Getúlio Vargas Foundation, an M.A. in International Business, and I'm a smart learner. Real estate and commercial growth are on the hot burner and fast tracked for Brazil. I would be part of that. That's where you come in. You may have not thought about it, but you are uniquely positioned to be the cultural attaché of your country in Brazil. (Don't fall over.) It is an appointed position, you don't need to go through all that falderal of the Foreign Service Exam (we know all about that stuff through the connection of Brazilian History, Rui Barbosa's career and fame in Brazil as an international diplomat and my Dad's business and government dealings.) Now, there are many, many marriages with U.S. business leaders or diplomats and Brazilian girls, almost all from the upper class. We, 'caro Miguel,' could do that. My father can get you that appointment. I want you to go back to Lincoln, do some research and hard thinking, and next year we can take up where we are leaving off. Pardon the worn cliché, we've both 'tried on the merchandise' and unless I am sadly mistaken, it was a perfect fit. Before we leave in a little bit, I want your reaction and see if we can really consider the matter. I know it seems outlandish, particularly on our first 'date,' but you've got to live the moment; who knows if this moment and time and everything could come together again. But me in the company, you Cultural Attaché, that's a nice thought."

I took a long swallow of champagne, tried to gather my thoughts, and could see she was waiting for some reaction. "Sônia, I'm in a bit of shock. It's too much like a Hollywood movie, love at first sight, rich girl meets poor boy, all that. I don't know what else to compare it to, oh yeah, there are a few 'Cordel' stories like this, but the girl is the daughter of an evil rancher - 'coronel' and the guy is a cowboy. Ha. I guess I am a bit of a cowboy, make that a 'lavrador' [farmer] coming from Nebraska. I think you have thought about this for a while, but porra! Let's slow down a bit and see what you've said and how crazy it seems to me."

Sônia responded, "Miguel, you are right. It seems crazy. And we are just beginning to know each other. I've had my eye on you, have seen your background and research and steadiness and perseverance at the Casa. So, for now, let it all rest, but don't forget my words and give us a chance."

26

THE RIO – NITERÓI BRIDGE - DANCING TO THE TUNE

We parted the Othon, friends, no more. I admit my head was reeling, but I needed to get to Chico's for rehearsal that Friday and the concert the next week. Rehearsal was upbeat, after all, Glória and the Soldiers' Monument had gone well. We played the "Mistakes of Our Youth," did the "Asa Branca" and "Pedro Pedreiro" segment, and Chico and the band did all the samba. Chico said he anticipated much the same on Monday, but with a wild and different venue. "No escape from the bridge! It's a first for all of us and maybe all Brazil. Let's hope the weather is good, the forecast said it will be unsettled. There will be a military presence, and the question is who in the crowd will show up. I think we need to persevere. See you here Monday morning, we'll load up the van in the a.m., drive to the bridge, set up and start at 1:00 p.m. "P'ra frente Brasil, por enquanto."

Before I knew it, Monday had arrived. "O Globo" had a headline about the concert, "Repórter Esso" the nightly national TV news featured it as well. The atmosphere was upbeat, hope for the future. I spent the weekend getting caught up on some sleep and psyching myself up, nervous time as usual for the non-professional musician and performer. The old rock n' roll was easy to review in my mind, the rest "Let it fly." For a change there were no women on tap, no surprise appearances of Heitor Dias, so I wrote letters home to the family in Nebraska, and even to my boss at U. of Nebraska, bringing them all up to date. And maybe more important, the draft of the next "Letter" to James Hansen. Dona Júlia said she was too old to fight the crowds but assured me she would watch all the reporting on TV, hoping those "cafajestes" ["sons of bitches"] in the military would not screw up or the "crazies" on the Left. Me too.

Monday rolled around, all the pre-concert stuff as planned. The weather was cloudy, an occasional bit of sunlight, but with gusts of wind. The crowd was already beginning to gather, a good sign I guess, at both ends of the bridge, but more so on the Rio entrance. The police knew we were coming, opened a path, and we drove out to the middle of the damned bridge. I had crossed it before on a bus, but standing there in the middle, the wind blowing and the bridge slightly swaying (even though it's made of a zillion tons of concrete) made me feel a bit of vertigo.

THE RIO DE JANEIRO – NITERÓI BRIDGE

(For readers of my next "Letter" a few details: Brazilians dreamed about the bridge since the late 19th century, but actual construction began under General Costa e Silva of military and dictatorship fame in 1968, thus among the "projetos faraônicos" of the regime, all debated in Brazil. Incredibly beautiful but scary, eight plus miles long across the not so blue waters of Guanabara Bay (porpoises still swim despite the pollution), five and one - half miles over the water, and, gulp, 236 feet high at the middle span for all the cargo ships to pass under. The dream and construction were all worth it, eliminating maybe the worst commute in all Brazil! That is, excepting rush hour in São Paulo. But as always in the "accidental" country of Brazil, there are great anecdotes, the best by Luís Fernando Veríssimo in one of his hilarious "crônicas" [chronicles] when he tells of the long delays caused by peons giving change at the toll booths. No one ever had the correct fare, and no one had change, so they began giving change in "balas" or hard candy! The problem was no one could make up their mind as to the flavor – orange, lime, apple, cocoanut! Enough said. I don't know if the candy story is true but it's likely. Oh, and it didn't change the habits of the bus drivers; one actually flipped over the side barrier, killing all aboard. But "Pra' Frente Brasil!"

We started on Brazil time, about a half hour late, the sound was about twice volume what it was supposed to be but Felipe (Chico's sound guy) wanted to take no chances. We all had chairs in case wind or vertigo got to be too much. I used mine. The crowd didn't seem to mind, thousands of 'cariocas' in blue, green, yellow shirts and some waving the Brazilian flag, danced in the traffic lanes. I think it added to the sway but maybe not. Chico did the same introduction as at the Soldiers' Monument, "Mistakes of our Youth" went well (all seemed to know the words in English, amazing!). He asked how many "nordestinos" were present. Not many, (there was a 100 cruzeiro admittance fee), but he recovered saying, "This is why the government is doing the projects, to get you jobs and a better life! I know it's on the radio and TV so I hope some of you are listening or watching."

There was an armed presence, guards from the PM, military police, with body protection, belly clubs and pistols, but they were cool and even danced along with the crowd. I can't be for sure but I think I saw Heitor Dias in his white linen suit, and a whole passel of folks from the Casa, even the stodgy ole' philology professor, and the girls! I don't know who knew what, but Claudia and Sônia were side by side. I gave a wave to all and heard a loud "Arretado, Arretado!" in response. Chico and the band were halfway through the samba segment when the skies opened up, pouring rain but luckily no lightning. But hey, all our equipment was electric, run on a big generator. It all cut out. And the wind came up. Cariocas are used to winter storms and rain, so out popped hundreds of umbrellas and shouts of "Não faz mal. Vamos pra' frente" [No problem. Let's go!]. So, they finished the concert with a backup generator, not nearly as powerful, a lot less loud, but it did the trick. Chico thanked the crowd, shouted a few "Viva Brasils" and said, "Sorte até agora, mas não vamos tentar os deuses maiores. Chau. Viva o Rio! Viva Niterói! Viva a Ponte!" ["We've had good luck up to now, but let's not tempt the weather gods. Bye.

Long Live Rio! Long live Niterói! Long live the Bridge!"]. We were all soaked, but "graças a Deus" no one fell off the bridge and there were no problems.

After we had packed up, turned the van around and were heading off the bridge on the Rio side, escorted by a cadre of motorcycle police, there was suddenly a loud bang, some kind of an explosion off to the side of the ramp onto the bridge. Police and soldiers converged out of nowhere (Heitor Dias was evidently not spoofing me a few days earlier). But after all the hubbub the escort regrouped and we headed on back to Jardim Botanico. Chico got on the phone right away, checked with Goeldi's office and got an "all clear," but with an admonition. "You're very fortunate; one small explosion and no organized protest or banners didn't upset us too much. It might have even been a blowout, not unheard of, hein? ["huh?"]. It could have been different. In fact I'd say it was all a huge success. You said the right words, the crowd appreciates our (ha) bridge. Rest up, it'll be different out at Itaipu next week. We'll be in touch soon with some plans for you."

After a few drinks and a lot of laughter, a heads-up for Friday rehearsal (we would fly out to Paraná State and Itaipu on Saturday) I said my goodbyes and headed back to Dona Júlia's where she was bubbling over again with enthusiasm for having "Arretado" as a boarder, a big change from her all-business normal demeanor, cussing out the military and everyone else during dinner hour in that first year I stayed with her in 1967. I could tell she had a lot of questions yet, but demurred for whatever reason, saying, "I guess you need to rest up (meaning more women on tap the rest of the week)."

The reason I haven't written more about what was going on in Brazil was because there was a hiatus in the news, no bombs thrown, no bank robberies, just off-season Escola de Samba [Samba School] rehearsals to make money from the tourists, and no real research to be done for the moment. That left the beach, but not without company. Sônia had my number, called, and said we should hit the beach on Wednesday, but not Copacabana. She would pick me up, my decision, in front of the Othon (I did not want to take a chance for an accidental encounter with Cristina Maria down the street from Dona Júlia's, or that matter, for anyone in her family). She said, "Look for a black Mercedes, four doors, me in front, 9 a.m. sharp, tá? I want to show you a real beach out on the Barra. We'll have dinner afterwards and get a chance to talk." I agreed, a bit hesitant to know what to say after our last and first date. But, hey Gaherty, live for the moment. I had bought a new "sunga" for the occasion, that Carioca skimpy men's swimsuit, a good time to try it out. I'm still fairly skinny so no beer belly to deal with. Sônia said we could change in the family's condo "getaway" (as if they needed one with the luxury apartment taking up one floor of the skyscraper near the Fort on Copa).

27

GAHERTY'S CATHOLIC TOURISM

INTERIOR OF THE SÃO BENTO MONASTERY

Let's see, this was to be Wednesday, so I took off on my own Tuesday, doing some Gaherty family Catholic tourism in Rio, places I had been before but felt some weird need now to revisit. Strangely enough my connection to the old 16th century Benedictine Monastery on the hill next to the port in old downtown Rio was the first thought. Dona Júlia had a friend, I don't think a confessor, one of the monks at the place, who acted as confident and helped her cut through Brazilian bureaucracy a time or two. He was my ticket. I had been with him for the silent lunch in the refectory two years before and a private tour later. Dom Eugênio remembered me, had actually witnessed from one of the second story windows from afar all the commotion on the bridge the day before, and I'm not sure how with all the vows, knew about Chico, "Arretado" and the concerts. He welcomed me once again to the refectory lunch and then a long talk in his office afterwards, what ended up as one of those modern confessions by you know who.

I was once again taken aback when I rang the buzzer on the front door of the Monastery, asked for Dom Eugênio saying I had an appointment, and was told he would be with me shortly. The middle-aged monk in full Benedictine attire came in a bit, shook my hand and said, "I remember you Miguel, a good Catholic young man, exemplary in your conduct with us. Welcome back, lunch in the refectory is not for fifteen minutes, so we have a bit of time to catch up. If you would, since we here are all limited in time with lay people, kind of fill me in on you since the 1967 visit. I'm assuming you are in the state of grace or would like to be, ha ha."

"Dom Eugênio, I'm hoping I still merit the visit, although like any red-blooded young man, I can admit some dalliances not exactly monk-like since we were together. In a nutshell I'm now an Assistant Professor of Spanish and Portuguese at a good public university in the United States, am back to Brazil to attend a high-powered Congress sponsored by the Casa de Rui Barbosa, but am a bit sidetracked with an unexpected part playing in Chico Buarque's performances. And I have given in to some temptation with moments with four Brazilian women. Maybe we can talk of all this after lunch, I'd really like to go to confession to you as well."

"Miguel, God is love and God is all forgiving. I on the other hand, between you and me, would enjoy a bit of talk of you out here in our 'real world' of Brazil. We can take an hour after lunch, I'll forego the usual nap, I think a good thing under the circumstances. Shall we sit down for a few minutes in the main nave, I'll whisper you a bit of History and perhaps you can quiet yourself, let God enter your heart, and then we'll go to the refectory for lunch."

Somehow or other lights were turned on, whereas before the church was exceptionally dark. I had been allowed to take photos in 1967 so there was no need of that, but that dazzling interior did prove both a distraction and a calming effect on me the next few minutes. Gaherty kept his mouth shut for a change. Father Eugênio gave me the "short course" in the history of the Monastery and its role as both seminary and instructive in the famous "Colégio de São Beneditino." I'm sure he had told the story a thousand times: the founding of the monastery as a result of a gift of the land by prominent Cariocas back in the 16th century, the construction over the next 100 years. Benedictines from Bahia were the original benefactors in 1590 and went on to plan and manage the place. Like other major orders in Brazil at the time, the Benedictines had land, and a lot of it, sugar cane plantations in nearby Nova Iguaçú and adjacent places. It enabled them to plan and construct what still today is one of the most beautiful churches in Brazil. In contrast to a deceptively simple Mannerist façade, it is the interior that is, once again, dazzling. The entire main nave, altar and ceiling are gilded gold, with beautiful stained-glass windows high above the altar. Statues of St. Benedict, Saint Scholastica and other Benedictines added later fill the church. The two baroque, rococo angels on either side of the altar are no less beautiful. Eugênio spoke briefly of the "Colégio" rated the top secondary school in all Brazil with famous graduates including Heitor de Vilas Lobos of "Bachianas Brasileiras" fame. He was just getting warmed up when a chime was heard, and he gently took my arm and guided me through what seemed like a maze to the Refectory.

It was a tall, airy (tall windows from the colonial construction open to the sea), and totally exempt from art or architecture except for a single Crucifix hanging in the center, a statue of St. Benedict to the right, and a speaker's pulpit on the left. Silence was the rule, the only sound that of a young Benedictine reading Scripture during the lunch. The Benedictines, at least those I saw today, were not starving to death. Food was very simple but bountiful, rice and beans, bacalhau [cod fish] and boiled potatoes, green beans and wonderful baked bread. Water to drink. No wine present, but I did think how an icy Brama Choppe or Portuguese white wine would have not been a bad idea. Mea Culpa. And I had a flashback to the São Francisco Church in Bahia, large but no less beautiful than São Bento and all its lascivious angels. Mea Culpa again. Lunch time passed quickly although I don't recall much of the scripture reading, done in a clear Portuguese by a young monk, maybe a novice or seminarian. Mike the language teacher got caught up more in the peroration than the message. There were about forty monks in the room, many very old men, a few of middle age and a few young ones. All wore the Benedictine dark habit, long, black, with front reaching to the floor and the cowl, currently pushed back from their heads, most with beards. I found myself thinking and wondering why I was never asked by the Jesuits to consider seminary, this while an undergraduate at Georgetown. Must have been because I could not get myself up for daily mass, not a good sign.

More important than all this may have been our conversation in Eugênio's quiet room on the residence floor above the refectory. He said, "Miguel, my time is yours, you seem to have wanted this moment. Since Vatican II, we think of confession as reconciliation, and instead of that dreaded wooden box with screens, we sit in comfortable chairs (not in this case, straight back and of hard wood), and converse. I will ask you the formulaic phrase before we get started, "How long since your last confession?"

Confession is sacred and private so no details on that (and not for "Letters" either), but I did tell the padre I was a Catholic "cherry picker" on doctrine, missed Sunday mass often even though I enjoyed the outdoor one on the end of Copacabana on Sunday evening with all the chicks. He smiled and said, "I know. That's a 'Pra' Frente' modern mass by one of the new 'progressive' priests, modern hymns which seem like samba to me, not exactly our style here at São Bento's. Go ahead."

I told him because of my interests in folklore, of the Northeast, of all I knew of Brazilian history and the treatment of the poor by the landholders, that I looked in favor on the modern Jesuits (I told him of my student formation, 7 years in Jesuit University), Dom Hêlder Câmara and "the worst violence is hunger." And my approval of the new Base Communities, the progressive church's "preference for the poor." Then I did admit all the fun times the last year or two with Brazilian women, including the sex, but could not guarantee it would not happen again. "So does all this make this conversation meaningless?"

He said, "Miguel, that depends on you. If you have sincere sorrow about it. It would be well for you to look back into some of that history you studied, recall the Jesuits' Missions and all they did to save the Indians in the name of the Church, but that they did enrich themselves (Jesuits were not allies of any of the other major religious orders and that included the Benedictines). And to remember the aim of Marxism and Communism with its atheistic beliefs is to destroy or replace all before them; that includes class society, most of Modern History, and the Church. There are many such people in Brazil today. My simplest defense of all this is to read the Lives of the Saints; two thousand years of sacrifice, good works and even death cannot be denied. Theirs was and is still a good cause. I'm aware of our sad history of the Spanish and Portuguese Inquisition, do not deny it, but also I cannot deny all the good works the church has also done. I mean following Christ's admonitions of feeding the poor, caring for the sick and the rest. As for your dalliances, I could say, 'Go and sin no more' (a smile and a chuckle); I'm sure that would fall on deaf ears. You are young, healthy, the flesh is weak. God is loving and God forgives, but there is a reckoning. My advice is to not forget us, remember we are here for you, and so are the sacraments." He blessed me, uttered the words of absolution and said, "I'm not supposed to, but I will sneak a look at 'O Globo' to see how you are coming along in your current adventure. May it and you go well." I said a simple thank you, shook his hand and went on my way. There was as always back to much younger days some sense of relief after the "confession," but short and tempered. Brazil got in the way of that. I had intended to do "2 for 1" that day, visiting the equally beautiful 18th century Igreja da Glória on the hill downtown, but no time. I did not think of Sônia all this time, a pat on the back for me? But I have to admit on the bus home she and the next day were on my mind. Hypocritical? Insincere? I don't think so.

28

BARRA BEACH

So, it's 9:00 a.m. on Wednesday and I'm out in front of the Othon again (Cristina Maria and the "Fusca" [Volkswagen 'Bug'] a year ago, but not "déjà vu all over again")." This is different. A shiny, black Mercedes sedan pulls up, beeps the horn, and I climb in, not without notice of the bellboys at the Othon. Mercedes are fairly rare in Brazil, some trouble due to Germany and Brazil's respective tariffs. So they are a big tag deal. I got in, leaned over for a kiss from Sônia and said, "Did you leave the Rolls Royce at home? Why are we slumming it in the damned Mercedes?" She answered, "Don't laugh; Daddy has one of those in a garage in London. But the "Fusca" doesn't have enough room for all our beach stuff. Why? Do you want to get out?" "Naah. I'll tag along."

We drove quickly to the end of Copacabana, crossed the streets over to Ipanema, drove down to the canal, turned right, drove around the Lago Rodrigo de Freitas, then under that long, long tunnel under Corcovado, into the North Zone and through streets I don't know on out to the Barra. Sônia said the 101 highway around Dois Irmãos at the end of Leblon is prettier, but this is tons quicker and that we might take the scenic route on the way back. After driving through Barra commerce, the only main street, we reached that long straight beach with all the tall condominiums (with gated entrance) facing the water. I told Sônia, "Don't get me wrong, but I'll take Copa or Ipanema, even if Cariocas say it is 'polluted' with the middle class. This is like being in another country or another planet." She got a bit huffy and said, "I've never said it was polluted. But smart ass, I'm sure you

98

don't know this part of Rio. It will make a good chapter for your 'Letters,' minus of course certain details." She laughed.

We pulled up in front of what seemed like a zillion story high, shiny new condo or apartment building, an iron gate in front. Sônia rang the buzzer, said something rapid in Portuguese I did not catch, the gate buzzed, opened and we drove into a huge underground parking garage. Lights went on automatically, a uniformed fellow rushed out, said, "Oi, Senhorita Rodrigues," gave me a knowing look, grabbed all our stuff and hustled us into a private elevator. Dark, wood paneled, mirrors on three sides, it whisked us up 25 floors to what must have been the penthouse. It was still in the a.m. But the curtains were drawn. Sônia quickly walked across a huge sunken living room and opened them. It was dazzling – bright blue ocean, white sand beaches in either direction, the window to Rio's south and southeast coast on down to São Paulo and Paraty in the distance.

She disappeared into one of the bathrooms and came out with a carioca bikini fairly well but not completely concealed under one of those beach coverings the women wear, a big straw sun hat, beach sandals and big towels. She said, your turn, and laughed. So I peeled off street clothes, squeezed into my 'sunga' with a t-shirt on top, a carioca beach hat I'd bought from a vendor in Copacabana, and sandals. She said, "Good try Miguel, but you'll never look like a carioca. You need to get a tan, but I've got sun block for your white gringo skin. Roberto (a 'butler' for such occasions) will bring everything else down. We'll have a cooler with plenty of water, a beer or two and some snacks, beach mats and an umbrella. 'Bora. [Let's go.]"

We took the service elevator down (for beach goers covered with sand and for the maids), walked across a beautiful tiled terrace with a large fresh water swimming pool, through a gate (once again with a guard) and right out in front to the sand. She said, "Here, I'll show you how a carioca goes to the beach." She made two mounds of sand just with her feet, put the mats carefully down, the idea being to lie down facing the morning sun and looking back toward the pool and the high rise. Roberto planted the umbrella between, two beach chairs to the side and the cooler. Then the real show began. I've been through this before! When Sônia peeled off the beach top and revealed that perfectly toned carioca body in a bright blue bikini top and bottom, the stallion was in the mare's corral again (pardon my much-used metaphor from times past). She made no secret she noticed and said, "I'm flattered. It's all right." She came up, rubbed those outstanding breasts up to my chest, put my arms around her where I quickly found the well rounded buns and gave me a very deep kiss. I said, "That didn't help any." We both laughed and ran into the surf with some pretty cold water settling me down. She still wanted the closeness and pulled me down in the surf and laid on top of me, moving her body to feel my erection, maybe just an accident. We both laughed and I said let's do some body surfing, the waves are perfect. Sônia turned out to be an expert, and I actually wasn't bad, having learned to "fazer jacaré" in past trips to the beach.

After a few minutes of that we walked back up to our spot, lay down on the mats, she opened the cooler and handed me an icy can of Brahma Choppe, a "limonada" for herself and said, "This sun will broil you," and commenced to carefully and expertly run the sun block over my entire body. I said, "That didn't help, again!" Me settling down, she said, "Now this isn't too bad is it? No one else uses this beach, it's private so you can relax, no pickpockets or sweeps from the favela kids on Copa or Ipanema, and we'll just take the sun for a bit." Okay by me, we probably just lay there for half an hour, and the sun in short doses does its thing, making you feel good all over. (I'm debating why I'm writing of all this, maybe a beach etiquette note for "Letters" but both of us incognito!) There was small talk, Sônia telling me about life here on Barra Beach, the setup at the condo, explaining why it was gated, just the "right" people around, but it still made me uncomfortable. I said, "This is a first for me, I'm enjoying the water, the sun, especially your company, but dammit I still don't feel right. It's not my scene Sônia, and I don't think it ever will be." She reacted, a bit huffy again, said I could get used to it, but after a bit said, "Chega! [Enough!] Let's go up and shower, have some great food, maybe even a little champagne, rest up and Ill drive you home." She didn't seem angry, but maybe disappointed with some issues dealing with this country bumpkin gringo. "I want to hear about your day yesterday and tell you about mine."

I held her hand (a peace gesture), and we retraced our steps back by the pool, now with several obviously upper class "cariocas" in beach attire (wow), under umbrellas, a few children frolicking in the pool, music from someone's radio, the whole scene. We were whisked up to the penthouse via that service elevator; I could see why, with all the sand. Sônia said, "Will you join me in a nice warm shower to get that sun block off?" It turned out to be a little more than that, mutually beneficial you might say, slow soaping up, then a cool rinse, but with lots of touching here and there and giggles and laughter. It evolved to drying each other off, a glass of champagne and a roll in the hay. We were indeed getting used to each other and laying relaxed and a bit tired on the cool sheets. Sônia said, "You must be hungry. I'll call room service and we'll chow down (all of these terms in Portuguese are more interesting, but no need to add to the "flavor" of it all).

There was a sumptuous 'almoço,' meaning the big noon meal in Brazil. "Maionese" [potato salad], fresh garden salad, "peixe, camarão" [fish, shrimp] and small lobster, and champagne from the frig. Sônia said, "Now let's talk." Uh oh. "You first, I want to hear about your day yesterday." I gave her an abbreviated version of São Bento, that is, all except the "confession." She was impressed and happy. "I knew you were down deep a Catholic, and with good taste. It does not get any better than São Bento. I guess you know some of our most famous people, particularly from the arts, graduated from there. How does that mesh with your Jesuit years? Daddy went to the Jesuit Prep here in Rio but did all his business training at the Getúlio Vargas Foundation, that is, all he needed; most was on the job for the last twenty years. I've talked a great deal about you to him, mainly your whole story – farm boy, Jesuit undergraduate and Ph.D. and professor at Nebraska. He had never heard of the latter, you know how it is here, Harvard, Yale, Stanford. But he had heard plenty about Georgetown and wondered with your background why you weren't in the State Department. Which leads me to our previous conversation a few days ago."

"Sônia I still think you are way ahead of me on this. Something in my gut tells me it would never work out. I've had other chances, not so glamourous, to stay in Brazil, make a life here."

She interrupted, "I know about Cristina Maria and the Ferreiras. The security for Rodrigues Limited checked you out; they have connections to the DOPS, and Heitor Dias was glad to talk some, knowing there would be a good word sent to his boss. Please, please don't get angry with me. For him it's just 'business.' For me, it's the future. Maybe you can appreciate how serious I am about you to do all this. I'm just saying I know all about you. I've had a couple of close calls with 'noivos' the last few years, all wanting a good job and money more than me. I know you are different, but I had to know if there was any competition." She held both my hands when she said this and seemed to think it might help.

"I think I'm really 'puto da vida' [super pissed off]. But then, what's one more watchdog after the DOPS? (Sarcasm). Porra, Sônia. If you would have asked me about my past love life here in Brazil, I would have been glad to tell you. I'm wondering, if we were married, would the same scrutiny be a part of it all? Let me cool down a bit, let's get our stuff together, you can drive me back to the Othon, and we'll put some time and space between us, maybe like you said, thinking about it in Lincoln."

I guess that did it; she began to cry, even sob. "Miguel you don't know the pressures in my life, with my family, the whole situation. I'm 25 years old. I am not a happy girl. I thought you would make me happy. I believe you are a miracle (I pray every day to St. Maria Aparecida). But I had to take this chance because you really are too good to be true – a good person with many virtues, I've never met anyone like you before. Can you forgive me? The 'investigation?' I meant well. I don't know what else to say. Let's make love again and make up. You've got to know I am a good person as well and only wanted the best for both of us."

So we did. More passionate than last time. And I think she at least was consoled. Mike, the bachelor, remembered in a flash that other Maria Aparecida, but it was just a thought. It did not interfere with the moment. Sônia said afterwards, "It can't end like this. Talk to me Miguel."

"I am convinced your heart is in the right place. I forgive you for all the checking up on me, still don't like it, but I forgive you. Do you have any idea how unreal all this has been to me, mainly for all the things in my life you already know? It's overwhelming. Life seemed too simple before. And home and Lincoln and maybe a call to Molly sound good to me now. Look, I'm going ahead with the 'gig' with Chico next week and then up to the Northeast. Then maybe we can talk, but at a neutral site, maybe the 'jardim' [garden] at the Casa de Rui. Okay?"

Sônia reluctantly agreed. I think she was very used to getting her way, and this had started in a pretty promising way. She smiled, but with a sad demeanor, said, "I guess you're right, but I'll hold you to that talk at the Casa. And I'm not making any other plans."

We drove back to Copa to the Othon, not saying much along the way. She stopped at the parking in front of the hotel, squeezed my hand, and we exchanged a light kiss. There were tears in her eyes and I felt like crap. Damn! Brazilian women! My Irish American momma would say, "Mike, what a fine kittle of fish!" I said goodbye and said, "Sônia, this was wonderful. You are a fine person and one luscious 'caricoa' as well. We'll talk after João Pessoa and the last concert."

29

THE FALLS AND THE MUD AND DUST FIASCO

Damn! Too many complications and too much going on. I don't even know what I did Thursday, maybe hanging out and going to the bookstores in Copacabana, one of my favorite things in Brazil. That and eating again at the "Braseiro" near the beach. I found myself in a taxi the next morning heading over to Chico's and the rehearsal. Everyone was in an exceptionally good mood, hardly believing all had gone so well so far with the "tour," especially Chico, maybe thinking too of the 'cachê' - the checks he received from Philips for putting it on. Same program, same rehearsal along with some muttering, everyone tired of the same ole' stuff, but Chico explained there was no chance to vary it due to the agreement with Goeldi and the government.

"Porra! Enjoy yourselves, Monday we're headed out to an amazing place. We'll fly into Foz de Iguaçu and take a van over to the dam. If we get a chance we can get in a visit to the Falls at Iguaçu; I've been there and it's one of the wonders of the world. Miguel, have you been there? On the other hand, if we leave tomorrow, we can do the visit before the concert, can you people be ready? Just a call to the Philips agent before we break up today and they'll set the whole thing up." Amazingly enough no one had been to Iguaçu other than Chico and everyone said, "Topo" ["Agreed"]. Chico added, "I'll get us reservations, a suite at the old Cataratas Hotel, great swimming pool, bar, great food, and then the trail along the Falls. So, it's travel to Iguaçu tomorrow, the falls in the p.m., maybe some 'farra' [partying] at the hotel, and the drive to the dam site on Sunday. We set up, do the concert in the p.m. and back here Sunday night.

I was very excited, got all my stuff together and met the group at Chico's the next a.m. Within an hour we were to Rio's downtown airport Santos Dumont and a charter flight to Foz. We actually saw the falls from the air before we landed, touted as the largest waterfall in the world! In spite of seeing photos and newsreels of the place before, it was astounding and wonderful. A van took us to the hotel, along with some hubbub, full of tourists yet lots of people knew the "famous" Chico Buarque and band would be checking in. My cohorts were all used to this, signing autographs on the way in, and even a few people knew about "Arretado" so I got out the BIC and signed a few. We got special treatment and were checked into our rooms on the top floor, one side with a few of the spectacular round swimming pool and lush, tropical foliage, the other with a view of the Falls. What made it for me was the buffet almoço – almost like American food back home – a welcome change from other Brazilian food, pardon me. Roast beef in gravy with mashed potatoes, good veggies, icy Brahma Choppe, and best of all, the first and only time in Brazil – lemon merengue pie! Another difference, I thought maybe I was in Europe, the wait staff all Caucasian, tall and speaking a Portuguese with an accent I had never heard. They said "falarrrr" almost the English R. I overate, stuffing myself, and needed a nap, but no time to rest; we all trooped out together and started the walk along the trail next to the Falls.

IGUAÇU FALLS

It's hard to describe, first because of the immensity, secondly the total scene – coati mundis begging along the trail, all kinds of tropical flowers and plants I had never heard of, hummingbirds all about, and then the Falls. You follow this long trail, viewpoints all along the way, each different because they wind in and out on the edge of the Falls. And the noise was overwhelming – millions of gallons of water coming down from maybe two hundred feet up, mist everywhere. I won't go on, but one viewpoint had a rickety wooden stairway down to river level and an even more rickety walkway right at the edge of a broiling and roaring river. They provided ponchos for all of us to not get wet from the mist. I think maybe it was the most spectacular thing I had ever seen. And that wasn't the best. Climbing back up at one point the trail veered out and you looked to the left to see the "Hell's Mouth," the horseshoe shaped end of the falls with the largest amount of water coming over the side and crashing down to the rocks below.

The trail continued, climbing now and we actually saw the huge wide river above the falls, with what is Argentina on the other side, specks of tourists seeing it from opposite us. The water was not clear in the river, brown because it was high water season. We were told you that for a price you could get in a tiny boat with an outboard motor, get into the river and they would take you fairly close to the edge. That didn't include a life insurance policy and a last will and testament. "De jeito nenhum! [No way!]." Chico said, "Next time. We've got work to do tomorrow." I'm thinking, "Wow. The dream continues. If it weren't for all this business with the band, I'd never get to see this." The late afternoon and evening promised more surprises and one helluva good time.

Back at the hotel everyone went for a swim and relaxed in a surprisingly warm sun, "caipirinhas" and beer flowing. The party went on after dinner, drinking, joking and carrying on in our suite of rooms. About 3 a.m. a bleary Chico said it's an early day tomorrow, so you "farristas" [party animals] better get some sleep." So be it.

ITAIPU DAM

At an ungodly hour, up at 4:00 a.m. and a good breakfast with plenty of hot, sweet Brazilian coffee, we piled into the van and drove for about two hours to Itaipu where the equipment van would meet us. Chico had said word was out that there were several bus caravans with dozens of buses from Rio and São Paulo, all the fans ready to make the 16 hours trek out to Itaipu. The concert was scheduled the same day at 3:00 p.m. Many buses were already present in the small, surprisingly shabby town a few miles from the dam, really a housing site for all the construction going on. The military were relaxing "normal" rules and would allow us to have the concert, not like on the bridge or even the Glória site, but out in the middle of what was the actual construction site. Security would be tight, full body searches just the same, I guess to be sure no one would blow up all the U.S. and Japanese huge earth movers and caterpillars.

We were escorted by military security to the dam site, another first for me and most of the others. I don't really know what to say, how to describe it, the total opposite of nature and all its beauty from the Cataratas. This was different from the previous two concert sites mainly because the dam was under early construction, and in fact it wasn't very pretty at all. You could see the incline up to what the first spillway would be. It probably was the military and Brazil's most ambitious project – a huge dam with 20 generators, the Paraná river behind it, but rerouted so all we could see was this huge oval inhabited by hundreds of huge earthmoving machines. The concert would be held in effect in the middle of that oval, dirt and mud around the edges. I guess Goeldi and colleagues just wanted Brazil to see the immensity of the plan.

I was frankly disappointed, impressed to be sure of the immensity of the project, and I think Chico was as well. I doubt that "nordestinos" were driving the huge caterpillars or earth movers, but there was a new 'favela' near the construction site with thousands of workers to do the hand labor when the big equipment was finished. Chico said, "Merda! I shouldn't have agreed to this, and I think it will be more of the same up in João Pessoa, the Transamazonic Highway is just getting started, but let's do it and get it over with."

It amounted to kind of a Brazilian Dust Bowl, the wind swirling around the stage, just a couple of thousand hardy fans in attendance. Chico gritted his teeth, gave a similar introduction to the ones in Rio, stating his hopes for success and employment for Brazilian workers. I'm cutting this short, maybe the reader can surmise, because it was one huge letdown. The program went well, fans cheered, but somehow, I think most everyone "estava na fossa" ["was in the pits"]. I think folks thought the dam construction was a lot farther along, and like me and the band, were disappointed. But it was the "dream" that mattered. The finished project would be the largest hydroelectric project in the world, produce more than the huge dam on the Yangtze in China and theoretically provide Rio and São Paulo with more electric energy than they could ever possibly need. "Por enquanto" ["In the meantime"]. I did have a thought; maybe Chico would let me do a solo with "Manhã de Carnaval" (one of the main songs from the movie "Black Orpheus," hauntingly beautiful) in João Pessoa. Ha. For sure the Cataratas and Itaipu would make the next "Letter."

The van ride back to Foz to the airport and the three-hour flight back to Rio were subdued enough. Quiet talk, no raucous laughter or fun. Maybe it was some kind of a sign of what we would meet at the airport in Rio. When we walked down the stairway from the plane, there was the roar of airplanes landing and taking off but of instant "vaias" [booing] and a few signs, looking like they were hastily painted, with "Vendidos!" [Sell outs!] "Chico não mais!" [Chico no more]. He said, "Puta que pariu! What the hell is going on?" We were hustled through the airport to our vans to take us back to the house at Jardim Botânica when we figured it all out. The newsstands with "O Globo" and "A Folha de São Paulo" had both papers with huge headlines covering half the front page,

FAMOSO JORNALISTA PRESO, TORTURADO E MORTO AO DEPOR AOS MILITARES EM SÃO PAULO

[FAMOUS JOURNALIST TAKEN PRISONER, TORTURED AND KILLED BY THE MILITARY IN SÃO PAULO]

Later we would read all the details. Iado Merzog was an immensely popular journalist in Brazil with all the right credentials. He was head of TV Cultura in São Paulo, an important news outlet in Brazil and a critic of the dictatorship. He also had ties to the Brazilian Communist Party. Called in for questioning of recent activities, something must have turned south; he was tortured and died. It amounted to murder. The DOPS showed his body hanging in a cell and pronounced it suicide. His appearance at DOPS headquarters in São Paulo and the facts leaked out and brought an uproar to any of what was left of the free press in Brazil, and really, the populace at large. The journalist who dug up the facts, already highly respected in Brazil, became a national symbol of the opposition. Already risking his life with the reporting, he was quickly moved to "most dangerous list" by the military and lived on pins and needles fearing his own safety.

There was no time to lollygag. Damn. The news hit us (and most of Brazil) like a ton of bricks. Protesters surrounded the airport exit, all silent but still holding the signs. I halfway expected rocks or stones to be thrown or worse. We were hustled into the vans, made our way home to Chico's place, almost ran into the house where he turned on the TV and began frantically to read the papers grabbed in a hurry in the Santos Dumont airport concourse. Full bottles of Pitú appeared from nowhere, bottles of beer and a couple people broke out their stash of "erva." The news could not have been worse. Chico's immediate reaction, "Chega! The tour's off. 'Por enquanto' turned out to be true. I'm getting on the phone now to Goeldi but in the other room. I'll let you know if a few minutes what's happening. Merda! Things were going so well."

In about fifteen minutes Chico came back into the living room, obviously shaken. "Goeldi wants to go on with the Transamazonic Concert in João Pessoa, all of us in good faith with the agreement. I said no way I could do that. He said then that we're back to base 1, all the conditions before – me being a good boy, not doing any anti-government stuff, and Mike, also base 1 for you. He counseled me to be wise and 'do the right thing.' Ha. Better get your bags packed. We meet him tomorrow downtown and it is not going to be pleasant."

Only an idiot could ignore all that. I did just as suggested; after leaving Chico's with his giving me a big "abraço," I got all my research stuff together and packed my bags. I was not up to any phone calls, to anyone, including Cristina Maria and the Ferreiras and certainly not to Sônia. Things were too tense and up in the air.

The next day I took the taxi to Chico's ready for the worst. He did not have much to say, just saying, "Arretado, it's been a good run. You have stood by me and I'll do the same for you today. Any shit that flies will hit me not you. Keep calm, don't talk out of turn, let's hear the General and then let me talk, okay?" I'm still a "guest" in Brazil at this point and don't want to screw up, so I said yes. Okay. A few minutes later we were on our way downtown, parked at the Censorship Building, now pretty familiar, took the elevator to the second floor, were greeted by the armed guard and ushered into the interrogation room.

General Goeldi and his assistant, both in full uniform this time, not the business suit stuff, welcomed us standing at his desk. No "abraços," no handshakes, all business. He then launched into a long speech: "Chico and Mike. This is extremely unfortunate, I mean the Merzog news. I realize we both were hoping for the best with the Concert Tour, and I recall your condition that 'por enquanto' ['for the time being'], all would be well. Remember it was you not me that had the idea for it all. I personally think that up through Itaipu all went well, fulfilling both our objectives. I'd like to ask you to put the Merzog news aside and finish the tour up at the Transamazonic in João Pessoa. It would be good for Brazil and good for you."

Chico responded, "With all due respect General, I, we in the band, I can't speak for Mike, can't do that. Thank you for the cooperation these past three weeks, but we can't."

The General stood up, frowned and said, "That my friend is the wrong decision. So be it. Just know that you are now back on our watch list. More than ever. We'll expect nothing – comments to the press, songs, concerts or the like – coming from you. I don't know what it will do for your career. It won't be good. You are naïve if you think the Left is still not a danger to us, the Revolution and to all Brazil. I'm confident most of Brazil will be with us. Merzog was a communist, a major voice of ill-conceived opposition to us. And he did hang himself after questioning and we'll never know for sure his real motive. I would say guilt and knowing there was no 'saída' [safe exit] for his actions. Again, consider yourself back on the 'watch' list; you never really were off it. Surveillance of all your activities will resume. Now a word for our friend Mike.

"I think for your own safety it would be best to go back to our plan of a few weeks ago. You are not officially being asked to leave Brazil, but we have arranged for your departure, let us know the destination and we'll make your reservations forthwith. I'll personally recall all the good moments this time around - the Philology Congress, your romantic social times we are all apprised of, and yes, the highly successful concerts with Chico - and all the positive things you wrote in the past and we hope for the future about our country. There are crackpots in Brazil just like in your country in all the protests of 1968 and 1969; we cannot guarantee your safety on the streets. So, thank you. What is your decision?"

"I'm truly sorry it all turned out this way. Chico had the best interests of Brazil in his heart and mind. Me too. I think I will fly to New York, have a conversation with James Hansen of the 'Times' and then head back to Lincoln. I've got time since I'm on academic leave this Fall to catch up on things, prepare for a full load of teaching next Spring, and do some writing. In spite of it all, I still love Brazil, its people and culture. Thank you, sir. And, by the way, do I have your permission to put 'Mistakes of Our Youth' in the next 'Letter?'"

"Fine, but only through Itaipu, and be careful of how you describe the latter, it is a work in progress you know."

Chico wanted to continue the conversation, but the General dismissed us withholding any further discussion with an impatient movement of his hand. He did shake hands with me, a very stiff version of the same with Chico talking in a Portuguese so fast I didn't catch a word of it and called the guard to allow us to leave.

In the taxi home Chico was fuming, saying he was sorry, that he had an inkling this might happen but was still hoping for the best, that is, until the Merzog affair. At home he got out the Pitú and beers for me and we had our last conversation. We both reminisced about my time in Brazil the past few months, all the reader already knows. Chico said, laughing, that he was glad I had that "bachelor's" experience with all the girls (he did not know a lot of the details, but knew enough). He said, "I never did hear about all the goings on you had during the Congress and can only surmise you worked in some fun. All I can say is that your idea for the Rock n' Roll and the rest brought me many moments of happiness." He said he had such a bad taste in his mouth from the General that he really was in no mood to relive it all. "You will always be a friend; we'll be in touch. I think I told you back in 1969 that I feared bad times ahead. Well, 'Arretado,' they have indeed come. Take care of yourself and remember us in Brazil."

I said, "Me too. It's all too much right now. I'm sorry I maybe spoke out of turn in the meeting, but hell it was the General who brought it on. I do want you to know that these past weeks have indeed been one of the highlights of my life. I'm taking the General's 'advice' and am going to New York tomorrow night, and I'm confident James Hansen will want a full report. I'll write a last 'Letter' but will be damned careful to not say or write anything that will jeopardize you or Marieta. But I won't be silent about Merzog and the storm I think is brewing. Just in case this all takes a turn for the better, I want you to let me sing and play 'Manhã de Carnaval' the next time we get together. It's the only Brazilian song I ever really learned and feel good about."

Chico laughed and said, "Certo, Arretado. Maybe we can do Carnival together sometime. And you can finally learn to dance samba." There was an "abraço" and a teary goodbye on both our parts. He said, "I'll be reading the 'Times' and I've got your phone number. Adeus."

I spent the rest of that day getting all my research stuff together, bags packed and all the small stuff that comes up. I called the Ferreiras and said things were happening, but I'd like to see them the next day. They said it was a priority for them so why not come for "almoço" and a drink. Jaime was doing the talking, and he added at the end, "Cristina Maria will be here, she does not want to miss this." All set for noon.

30

ALL BETS ARE OFF

That left the evening. I took a deep breath and called Sônia. She was almost ecstatic on the phone, "Graças a Deus you are all right! You should have called me 'Arretado.' Like everyone else I saw the news on that farce of a concert out at Itaipu and the Globo TV news clip of your van leaving Santos Dumont. But no news after that, anything could have happened. Later, and, pardon me, Rodrigues security knew about your appointment at Censorship with Chico this morning. Even my father, a staunch anti-Communist was upset about the Merzog news. He said, "Our country is not supposed to work that way. I'm thinking there will be some kind of reprisal from the Left and then all hell will break loose." Me, I'm more concerned about you, and by the way, us. I went home and cried the other day after you got out of the car after Barra. I've got to see you. What is happening?"

I told Sônia just that I would be leaving the next evening via Varig to New York, no more. She said, "Will you meet me at the Othon again tonight? Same place same time, but no complications on either of our part?" I thought for a while, said, yes, but that I was in no shape or mood for anything beyond conversation and maybe dinner. "Fine," she said, "but maybe I can cheer you up, rather, both of us. See you at 7:00."

Sônia was in the same spot at the tables as before. She waved when I came in and we sat at the table, exchanging a quick kiss. She touched my arm and said she was relieved I was all right and wanted to hear my latest. I filled her in, no point not telling the obvious: General Goeldi's formal request and advice that it would be best for me to leave Brazil, and soon. No hard feelings and hoping for the best (and a veiled notice to be careful what I wrote in "Letters"). I added that it seemed like good counsel and was preparing to leave the next night via Varig for New York.

She seemed pensive, saying "Can we have a last dinner together? I've got the suite key again." When I agreed she stood up, saying it's more discrete for talk in the room. When we were settled in that same place with that same view, she opened a bottle of champagne saying, "I think you could use some good cheer after all the events of yesterday." After more than one flute of the bubbly she said, "Miguel, I can pretty well see your mind is made up. One does not argue with the DOPS, Censorship and all the rest. Just think of all that has happened. You must feel like waking up from a dream, I mean the whole business with Chico and the band, the concerts and yesterday's news. You have my phone and I hope you will call me from Lincoln; if you don't call soon, I'll call you. If you want to come back to Brazil after you've got things settled in Lincoln, I can arrange all that, in spite of what you might be thinking about the government. I think you can see I don't give up easily, not after our time together and getting to know each other. Let's have a nice dinner, more champagne and then we can make our goodbyes."

So, it happened, a scrumptious fine dining meal by room service. Conversation was a bit stilted, but Sônia not so subtly plied me with more champagne. She talked about the latest from good ole' Dad. "He says it's time to join the company, that I've had my distractions. I think he hopes I'll forget about you. I'll start in the Contracts Office, the law degree maybe preparing me a bit for that. He thinks I can be just like him, learn on the job, grow with the company, and be a good choice for an ambitious young man who thinks like him. (She was almost in tears by this time.) I'm resigned to that now, but as you can see, not so happy about it. I'm planning on seeing you in a few months; we have business contacts all over the United States, but I'm thinking a rendezvous in San Francisco, and all on the company ticket. By then you will have had some time to get back to work, do your writing and teaching. For me, that's the best-case scenario. It's your turn."

"You've got it all right in my case. I want to get my feet back on the ground at the university. I'm still untenured you know but have some irons in the fire which should come to fruition the next year or two. I'm still the farm boy, blessed with the possibility of a great career, a lot going for me. My main interest in Brazil, in spite of 'Letters,' Chico and all the rest, is still Literature, still the poets of the 'Literatura de Cordel,' and writing on Brazilian Culture. By the way, if I can't come back to Brazil soon, and that appears to be the case, I'm still also a professor of Spanish and that presents possibilities of research and travel as well. So, I'll see. Life gets lonely in Lincoln but you know things can change; Molly is still in D.C. I haven't forgotten her. As for San Francisco, I'm not sure right now if that's a good idea."

"Mike, I'll give you some time, me too for that matter. But don't forget about me. Can we seal all this and make a memory for the two of us? We've got to make love tonight, now, and have you leave Brazil thinking of me. No conditions, no promises, just a final moment."

Against my better judgement I agreed, soon Sônia making me forget any doubts. It started in a tender way but soon warmed up to some pretty passionate sex. She seemed more beautiful than ever, that voluptuous 'carioca' physique in full bloom. But then it had to end. We both dressed, said our last goodbyes, both sad, but what can you do? I left the suite, took that elevator to the lobby and walked through the Copa streets, trying to clear my head, heading to Dona Júlia's, emotions astir. Final packing ahead, and the Ferreira's tomorrow.

31

GOODBYE TO THE FERREIRAS

I rang the doorbell at the Ferreiras noon the next day. Cristina Maria opened the door, gave me a quick hug saying, "Mike, you've got to have a story to tell and we all want to hear it. Come on in." Jaime and Regina were in the living room, both giving me a hug as well. Jaime ordered drinks and I said, "Jaime, get out that Johnny Walker Black, this calls for something a little stronger under the circumstances." They had all followed the news, like I said, it was all over the papers and TV Globo, but they did not know about the last "interview" with Censorship. Cristina was sitting beside me on the divan, but at the opposite end, Jaime and Regina in the easy chairs in front of us. The drinks came for both of us Jaime saying he would make an exception of Dr's orders and join me.

I made it short, hitting the highlights the reader already knows: General Goeldi's pronouncement of "back to stage one," Chico stifled, and me "invited" to take the plane out tonight. The Ferreiras were by now old friends, notwithstanding the times with their daughter. I owed all of them a lot, and the bond was certainly cemented now over four years. They were smart enough to read between the lines. What ensued was almost a family conversation. Jaime expected the worst vis a vis the Merzog revelation. He said that the tense atmosphere was almost palpable. "There is going to be reprisal; I'm not sure in quite what form. The Left is fractured but there are still powerful forces working out there. I would not be surprised with more bank robberies to finance them, maybe even more kidnappings. You were lucky you weren't a victim last year! I and my friends are lying low, I'm checking in at the business which by the way is doing well. We've got one of the many contracts to fill that mud hole you were in at Itaipu the other day. Cristina Maria is in Law School, the boys in Jesuit Prep. But frankly I'm more afraid for you right now. There are crackpots who would like to create a crisis for the government and doing harm to the young American in the middle of all it would not be an unlikely move. In spite of it all I think I'd contact General Goeldi and make sure you have safe conduct to the airport tonight. But, uh, don't call from here. Dona Júlias would be safe."

The conversation with Jaime Ferreira was like a year ago, like Yogi Berra would say, "Déjà vu all over again," but more ominous. After the serious talk we enjoyed another of those Brazilian dinners I was never ready for, "pato no tucupi" from Pará state again and a wine from the region. There was small talk, they wanting to know my plans back home. I repeated what I had said to Sônia, business as usual, checking in with the "Times" in New York and back to work in Lincoln, adding that for the unforeseen future there would be no more visits to Brazil. Cristina Maria was very quiet during the entire time but when I was ready to leave, she said, "Daddy and Mom, I need ten minutes in privacy with Mike." All seemed to understand that. We did the goodbyes, her Mom giving me an extra big hug (I thought) with some tears in her eyes. "Miguel, we won't be forgetting you." I hugged her again, gave Jaime a last embrace, saying I would be following events via the news and hoped for the best for all of them. Then I had that ten-minute talk sitting on the welcome bench with Cristina Maria in the foyer.

"Miguel, to think it all started with meeting 'Arretado' on the beach at Ipanema, then all those times we watched the MPB music festivals on TV Globo and you got to know about Chico Buarque. Porra! I never thought it would come to this. It all seems distant now, but our times are still an indelible memory. I've got the 'Mistakes of Our Youth' LP, including your part, and I'll be playing that until it wears out. Law School mid-terms are coming up, so that will keep me busy, but I want you to know there are many times, many, when you pop into my memory. And always good memories. Keep in touch with all of us." She hugged me, rubbed that wonderful body up next to me one last time and gave me a very deep kiss. I laughed, "Cristina, you did it again. Give me a few moments to calm down." She said, "Once good chemistry, always good chemistry. Adeus meu bem." I said, "And it's mutual. I won't forget you."

32

A Contradiction In Terms – Heitor Dias

I left the Ferreiras feeling pretty much drained. Back at Dona Júlia's I did make that call to General Goeldi. He assured me my taxi would be followed by his security, wished me well and hung up. There was little time before the taxi to Galeão Airport, but Dona Júlia and I had a final talk as well. I'm using the word final in everything. That's the way it seems. She was back to her 1967 self "xingando os cafajestes" [cussing out the bastards] in the military (even though General Castelo Branco was from her home state of Ceará), the bureaucrats running Brazil, even the street merchants robbing her in the local "feira" [street market]. Did I leave anyone out? In a way it made me laugh inside; this was the ole' gal I knew. She smiled, said "We're going to miss you. Who would have thought? I've never had a roomer who could stir things up as much. And stir me up! You even made me feel a bit young again. (The ole' gal turned a bit red.) Boa Viagem. But take care of yourself and pray for us here in Brazil." We had a quick hug, I gathered my bags and was out the door, down the elevator and the taxi was waiting.

As the 'carioca' taxi driver swerved through the evening traffic out to the Galeão I could not help but remember the last time a year ago and the kidnapping threat I only learned about in the airport. No problems this time. I was checking in for the overnight flight to New York, and history then did repeat itself, Heitor Dias walking up to me in the line. He said, "I'm not sure you will talk to me, but porra Miguel, we've got to part friends." I was in no shape to rail and end it all with any complications, after all, Heitor was still the DOPS first, a friend to me second. I said, "Heitor let's break routine and instead of a cafezinho have a stiff 'caiprinha' in the waiting lounge. I'm early to check in like all the gringos like you say. Você topa?" We went to the bar in that old favorite lounge with all the World War II airplanes on the wall and had our last conversation.

He started. "Miguel, first things first, I'm really sorry for how things have turned out, and I want to explain, not apologize, for Sônia's getting news about Cristina Maria. I could have told you if we had been together and it came up, but it didn't. There's not a formal link with Rodrigues Limited, but they are good customers of the government and can ask for information. That's what happened. I hope like hell it didn't screw up anything. That Rodrigues family is way too powerful for even the generals to ignore."

"Heitor, it didn't really change anything, but you can be sure I'll be damned careful next time, and it does not make me love Brazil anymore right now. But porra! I am glad to see you. It looks like this departure may be my last from Brazil, at least for the future as far as I can tell. It seems like a decade since that first time when you cornered me on the street in front of Dona Júlia's! Like you Brazilians say, "As águas rolam" ["Lots of water under the bridge"]. Anyway, I'm back to the U.S. soon and glad of it, a stop in New York tomorrow to talk to the 'Times' people (and maybe get a check, I could use it), and then a late flight to Omaha and on home. Drink up, the 'caipirinha" is on me."

Heitor did just that, commenting he would be off duty after talking to me. He seemed like one of those romantic Brazilians who liked to remember old times over drinks in a 'pé sujo;' well, in fact he was. He tried to make amends not only for himself but Brazil and seemed to get a thrill of talking over our encounters and past. "Arretado! I still like that. Do you realize you have made a very dull job really interesting! Between keeping track of you, and I liked the part with all the women, it sure has been different duty. Nossa! I even learned some things about my country I sure as hell wouldn't have otherwise. The Casa de Rui! Your shithead poets and their shithead poetry! I can see where the 'flatheads' like it. But most of all that whole business with Rock n' Roll and Chico Buarque. It's been quite a ride and I'll miss you. But, Miguel, don't look for any love letters from me or General Goeldi, and you better hope Chico has seen the light and will have a low profile. The word is we are all to be on high alert the next few days, really indefinitely. I think anything can happen and any day. Hey, they just did first call for your flight, wouldn't want you to miss that and maybe have to spend the night at Sônia's or hey even Maria Aparecida's. I forgot; she is really sad and disappointed you never showed up again. Maybe you can give me a message for her. So, chau, my gringo friend. Stay out of trouble, and oh, watch what you write. We will be reading the 'Times.'"

I said, "Heitor. All much appreciated. Tell Maria Aparecida I am extremely sorry. Maybe next time if there is a next time. I think of her every time Brazil celebrates that Saint's day. Maybe you can console her yourself, certo? Heitor, Brazil has been good to me, and it's not over. I'll be teaching those damned open and close vowels in Portuguese class, Brazilian Literature including your 'unfavorite author Jorge Amado' and writing about the latest events from 'Cordel.' Let's hope to God somehow Brazil comes to happier days. You are a scoundrel, but a good scoundrel; I won't tell anyone about the illegal Marlboros. And find yourself a good woman! Chau meu amigo."

This time Heitor gave me the big "abraço," the full works, and about squeezed the breath out of me. I picked up my carry on, waved again and headed to Varig check in. Funny what comes up in life; that same stacked Varig gal from Los Angeles (seems like an eon ago) was at the counter for the check in. She smiled, laughed, and said, "Wait here." A few minutes later she came back with the boarding pass: "O' Arretado. Você vai em primeira classe! É o nosso agradecimento pelo apoio a Chico." ["Oh, Cool Guy, you are going in first class. It's our way of thanking you for all the help you gave to Chico."] I was surprised but not enough to not thank her and give her a big "abraço" jointly returned. Then I was directed to check-in, placed at the front of the line and in a bit escorted to the front of the airplane. A first for me. But who is to complain? The plane was on time, we were all loaded, and it was good to get back to my usual travel routine – drinks, dinner, this time with all the accoutrements of first class. After an after-dinner liqueur and a fiery hot and sweet Brazilian "cafezinho," I began my long diary report. I can't sleep on airplanes and it would be an eight-hour flight, so there was plenty of time to remember, think and ponder the future. And thank God or my guardian angel (I always think of Riobaldo and Diadorim of "The Devil to Pay in the Backlands") for being safe once again, Gaherty the patriot heading home.

The travel notes report began with a careful reading of the lead articles in "O Globo" and "A Folha de São Paulo" over the Merzog affair and then settling down to a lot of thinking and writing (much of which would form the basis of my last "Letter" to the "Times"). Needless to say, I had to edit out the Gaherty personal matters – I mean the women and times I have already written about but not included in "Letters" – but there would be plenty to say about events since Itaipu.

The Philology Congress, all the contact and interaction with Chico Buarque, the music "gig," and the limited tourism made for a very successful trip. And renewing old friendships, in some cases, amorous! No need to repeat what I have already written, but the future was on my mind, that is, the connection with and work for James Hansen at "The Times," and settling back into routine at the university. I think there will be a lot of research and writing to come, but now based on my research library in the office in Lincoln, the newspapers and what I can learn from Brazil. Looking forward to New York in the morning.

33

JAMES HANSEN AND "THE TIMES" – A PLAN

The plane arrived at JFK at 8:00 a.m., a very bleary Mike on board. In spite of it all I might have slept four hours, good for me. I had my last airline breakfast on Varig, the highlight good Brazilian "café com leite." Oh, I forgot to say I had called James Hansen after the Goeldi dictum, asking for a meeting. He was pleased saying we had much to talk about, made me a reservation at the old rat trap across from Madison Square Garden and put me on his calendar for a one-hour meeting in the early p.m. "After you've had a nap and rested a bit from the jet lag. Jeeze, Mike you dodged another bullet, but great work!" There was a Gaherty sign at the baggage area, not expected this time by me, but an employee of "The Times;" he grabbed my heavy bag, caught a taxi out front and took me to the Hotel Pennsylvania across from the Garden. I checked in, set the alarm for noon and tried to sleep and succeeded for just a little. New York City was a shock as usual, although amazingly the drive in from the airport was not as jammed as I expected it to be, this after passing through the East River Tunnel and the skyscrapers of Manhattan ahead.

I walked, a good walk because I needed to stretch my legs, and enjoyed the New York big city bustle. Arriving to the snazzy "Times" building, I was whisked up the elevator to James Hansen's office, just a little before 1:00 p.m., right on time. Ushered into his office by the man himself, we shook hands, a shoulder embrace and ushered me into one of the easy chairs in the office, the same as last time on the 20th floor, corner office of course, with that great view of downtown Manhattan. I haven't said yet; the second book of "Letters" was now out, courtesy of the "Times," and James says it has done well, a different account than that long "Letters I" and shorter, maybe a good thing. "It has done well; there is a growing list of fans for Mike Gaherty's adventures! However, it is a whole lot spicier! Whose idea was that? I've told you to 'tell it like it is,' so no problems here. Your readers are happy you don't spend all your time in the libraries. I think your last two months now in 1971 are no less a draw, but we can talk about books in a bit. How about that drink of Glenlivit to celebrate your safe arrival? My God, we've followed your recent 'Letters' and it's like the French say, 'plus ça change, plus c'est la même chose,' ["The more things change, the more they seem the same"], but with a lot more spice this time. Heitor, the DOPS, General Goeldi, your great stuff on the Congress, the evolving story with Chico Buarque, and damn, the concerts and the Merzog story. Like I said before, this is a lot different from one of our stringer's account; I found myself looking forward to each new 'Letter.' I realize this year's batch was unsolicited, but you didn't need my permission; we printed the new ones right away. Now fill me in from your perspective, I'm all ears."

I must have talked twenty minutes without an interruption. Hansen would have his say when he was ready. I reviewed what the reader already knows, the beginning with the fall out of Molly and my plans, the Congress, the original time with Chico and the 'Letter' about his songs, and the serendipitous event of joint interest in Rock n' Roll, the concerts, and then Merzog. Leaving out the social moments with the ladies but talking of the reunion with the Ferreiras. James said that was pretty well what he knew from the "Letters," expressed his disappointment about me and Molly, saying he was not totally surprised, but then said he really wanted my take on Brazil, now and coming months.

"James, everybody I know and was with expects really bad times to come, Ex-Congressman Jaime Ferreira, Chico Buarque, Heitor Dias of the DOPS and even the landlady in Rio. This time the government crossed the line – Merzog is no small fish in the pond, and what he represents is paramount in Brazil – Freedom of the Press. I would love to meet and have you meet the São Paulo journalist who broke the story, and I'm hoping he has not been hauled in like Merzog, a real possibility. You and he are both courageous journalists, and no need to say you don't realize the gravity of the situation. My take is that Brazil is a ticking bomb waiting to explode or maybe not, only time will tell. For sure the government with AI-5 and censorship shows no signs of letting up, in fact General Goeldi intimated this is just the beginning. As for me, I'm officially out of the loop, 'invited' to leave Brazil and no invitations to come back."

James lit his pipe, took a swallow of the Glenlivit, seemed deep in thought for a while, kind of uncomfortable for me (So, I finished my glass). "Mike, I totally agree. What to do? I'd like a final 'Letter' pretty much saying what you just reported. Once again, careful, careful; we can't compromise Chico, Marieta, Jaime Ferreira, and the press in Brazil. Send it to me from Lincoln, I'll give it a careful read and let you know if any changes. But nor can the 'Times' forget about Brazil, especially now. I propose after you return to Lincoln, get back into academic life, that you continue to write your 'take' on Brazil. We'll have to change the title, not sure yet quite what, maybe 'Letters About Brazil.' We can pay you a stipend for your work, not as much as when you were in Brazil, more like an 'honorarium.' How does that sound?"

"Mr. Hansen, I would like nothing more than to follow your ideas and plan; I'll only know once I catch up on the research notes and documents I brought back with me, see what I can garner from the Brazilian papers (they come slowly and late to our library), and maybe, if I'm lucky, talk to Chico on the phone a few times over the next few months. I really doubt I'll be going back to Brazil for the near future. We don't know what will happen to the military, but right now, no one is in condition to end the dictatorship. A 'light' did go on during the flight home; I did have one different idea I'd like to run by you."

"Go ahead, you haven't disappointed me yet."

"My premise: travel and research in Brazil is over for the unforeseeable future. But life goes on. You know I teach Spanish as well at the university and have serious interests in Pre-Columbian sites in Mexico and Central America; in fact, I will be teaching, if they let me, our Spanish American Civilization Course at the U of N. If I get tenure and promotion and that's a big if, I'll apply for research and sabbatical in Colombia, a particular interest different from Mexico and Guatemala. Maybe we could do some kind of 'Letters' from there. I know it's just an idea, but as far as I know I won't be back to New York to talk to you in person, so I'm striking while the iron's hot."

"Mike, that's intriguing, but seems far down the road. We are beginning to get news of an entire new reality in South America, the drug trade, what they call the "Cartel," mainly in Colombia. But these people, pardon me, 'shoot to kill.' Sit on this for a while, let it percolate and in a year or so send me a proposal. As for the Pre-Colombian cultures in Mexico and Guatemala, we always have reader interest in that. I could see a special series on that part of the world. And, more importantly, I've got good friends at 'National Geographic' and could always put in a good word for you. Don't bother to buy a camera, I'm thinking of the write-ups for the Nikon people and archeologists. But that's just food for thought. Let's go ahead with this next year's emphasis on Brazil. Call me in a couple of months and let me know how it's going, we'll look at any new writing, and see. Mike, I just want to thank you for all you've done the past now three years is it? Damned good reading, and maybe it has helped our international circulation a bit. Not all bad. I've got another meeting coming up, a stringer reporting in on another ambassador kidnapping in Mexico City. No end to the excitement. Enjoy the rest of your day in town, get back to that Irish bar you like so much, and safe travels to the 'outback' (laughing) I mean Nebraska. And, oh, I hope your personal life takes a happy turn. You were sure about Molly when we last talked."

I walked back to the hotel, now late afternoon, decided to try the Irish bar, get a corned beef sandwich and a Harp and catch up on sports; fall football just around the corner. And the thought did cross my mind, would that "mystery lady" who was so much fun last time here show up again? The reader of "Letters II" might remember that colorful conversation. Too bad she didn't show, must have been too early for her "appointments." Ha. It might have saved me from some impulsive wrong decisions. Back to the hotel, final packing and the subway out to JKF the following morning.

34

REPORTING IN - NEBRASKA

The flight to Omaha was uneventful, welcome to the lousy airline service in the U.S., that is, if you are in coach! Arrived safely and caught the express bus out to Lincoln. I had mixed emotions, a letdown I guess from the past two plus months. It's difficult coming into a dark, cold apartment in Lincoln, Nebraska, after Rio de Janeiro and the tropics and all that went with it. What do they call it, attitude adjustment time? Next day was to be a return to campus, my office, a meeting with Dr. Hillardson, the Chair of the Modern Language Department, and seeing how I would keep busy until January and a return to teaching. An aside: since I was officially on department leave for the Fall term, no regular paychecks were coming in. There was a stipend check from the "Times," but it did not amount to much; it would be savings until January. It was now the end of September so three months without pay.

Doc Hillardson warmly welcomed me, poured coffee for us, smiled, leaned back in his chair and said, "Mike, wonderful to see you again. I think many folks here have followed your adventures in Brazil since July. I for one. The International Section of the 'Times' is always great reading for all of us. We got the request for the academic leave and covered your courses. It's a bit of 'déjà vu' I think from last year in 1970, but fill me in. Then I'll tell you what's new here, most of it good news for you. The U is still on the make for national prestige and I think you can be part of our forward movement."

"Dr. Hillardson, I'll try to make it brief, but it's one helluva story. First the academic part. It was a real honor and serendipitous moment to be part of that

'Primeiro Congresso de Filologia Portuguesa e 'Os Lusíadas' de Luís de Camões.' I represented U of N well. Important – during the Congress a seminal and major book on Brazil's 'Literatura Popular em Verso' [Brazil's folk popular poetry later to be known as 'A Literatura de Cordel'] came out with much fanfare. The Brazilians know how to have a big party along with a book signing. I have one of the chapters and am in the company of the major national scholars of 'Cordel.' I'm counting on that to help me when tenure time comes.

"After the Congress it was all a dream come true – important interviews with Chico Buarque de Hollanda and the relationship of his songs to 'Cordel' and my report to the 'Times.' The surprise and frosting on the cake was an unexpected but wild adventure with Chico, making LP recordings and actually playing and singing in some of his concerts. The latter would involve the indirect so-called sponsorship of the Brazilian Military, at least the 'permission' of the same. It all ended on a scary note – the revelation in the national and international press of the questioning, torture and in effect murder of a major Brazilian journalist. The consequences were a dictum for Chico to stop writing and performing and me being asked to leave Brazil. I know all the events with Chico have no bearing on my work here, will be a footnote to tenure, but the 'Letters from Brazil' I have done the last three years for the 'New York Times' will eventually be in three books by a major publisher in New York. That is amazing publicity for us here at the U of N. The Pernambuco book is "still in the works," but it will come out. So that takes me to the present with you and back home in Lincoln. On a sad note, my engagement with Molly in D.C. fell through, but who knows what the future may hold on that. Right now, it's not promising. I guess it will mean less distractions from work."

It was Dr. Hillardson's turn, "Mike, an amazing story. You are indeed unique in this department in a lot of ways. Glad to hear of the research results; they will stand you in good stead in a year or two for the tenure process. I'll expect you to get your teaching schedule set up for spring term, same duties as before with a split with Spanish and Portuguese. So, settle in and welcome home. I am sorry for the development with Molly, but perhaps that will get ironed out; I hope so. Thanks again and just know that I personally and most of us here are very happy to have you for a colleague. By the way I have a slush fund here for special occasions and I think your work, keeping in mind the unpaid leave, calls for some special assistance. I can help out with that; it won't make you rich but may help pay some bills until January."

I was moved by that, his good will and generosity, thanked him profusely and walked down to my office to settle in. A lot of thinking and writing was in store and then back to the reality of the classroom and more research. U of N here we go. First was the final "Letter" as promised to James Hansen – mainly my views on the immediate future in Brazil vis a vis the Merzog business. Then preparing anticipated classes for the spring term, probably Portuguese language courses, a Survey of Spanish Literature and possibly an upper division course on Chico Buarque's music and role in preserving free speech in Brazil.

35

NEW YORK, HANSEN HOSPITALITY AND MOLLY

A surprise call came from James in November inviting me to New York for a book signing for "Letters I" and "Letters II" for the New York Times Book Company. He said it would be a small affair but believed it would boost sales, backed by articles in the book section of the "Times," and offered airfare and lodging at the old Pennsylvania Hotel. It wouldn't be anything like that party at the Casa de Rui and the "Studies" book on "Cordel," but University of Nebraska professors don't complain. I quickly said yes and was off on November 7th to New York. Oh, another event and not unimportant at that, was possibly meeting Molly in New York for our first encounter since the break-up. That in turn was the result of a phone call I made to her from Lincoln right after Hansen's invitation.

When I called, I must admit I was full of trepidation. Molly answered the phone, not unfriendly but certainly neutral in tone. We talked for about fifteen minutes. I basically admitted that it had been back to "bachelor days" in Brazil, without going into any detail, and ended with describing plans for a return to academic life in Lincoln. I told her about the DOPS' final "invitation" to leave Brazil and said there really was no possibility of returning there for the near future, "Cordel" not reporting anything new, and the bleak political scene. Molly was quiet, receptive to listening at least. She did not volunteer anything about her own love life in D.C., only saying that work was going well and she was keeping busy. She did say that she followed the "Letters" in the "Times" of the last two months and in spite of everything was rooting for me and getting a kick out of the whole music affair with Chico and the concerts. She said she could read between the lines of my conversation and just assumed that I was not spending most nights alone in Rio. I then took a deep breath and asked her if she would come up to New York for the book signing, stay with me in the hotel but with me on the Murphy Bed in the tiny room, and have a conversation. Surprisingly enough she said she would think about it. I offered to pay her expenses, but she said no, not necessary, probably not wanting any "favors" from Mr. Gaherty. In fact, two days later she called, agreeing to the visit but basically saying, "We are not back to where we were. This is like one of your research trips – seeing what's going on, an "exploratory new beginning," but she did laugh after saying that, a good sign. We agreed to meet in the lobby of the hotel on a Friday evening; the book signing was scheduled for a tiny bookstore at the Village on Saturday, and she would be on the Amtrak back to D.C. Sunday p.m. She did say at the end of the conversation, "You didn't ask about me since the call. I'm a bit offended by that. I know you can be immersed in your own little world, academia, Brazil and all, but I'm hurt you haven't mentioned me and my feelings."

"Molly, I'm sorry once again. I can only say I was afraid to ask."

After what seemed an interminable flight from Omaha, a courtesy ride to the hotel from James Hansen, I arrived at the Pennsylvania, pretty excited about what was to come – geez, a book signing in New York City, but even more, a reunion with Molly. I checked in, went to the room and unloaded my stuff and back down to the lobby. There she was seated on one of those divans in that huge place. What can I say I haven't said before, a beautiful lady, auburn hair, green eyes, voluptuous figure, with a small overnight bag and it turns out a welcoming smile. We greeted each other with a hug and light kiss. Molly suggested we go to the hotel coffee shop and get reacquainted. Here's the gist of the conversation.

Molly opened with what I don't think was exactly an apology, soon to be followed by mine, maybe just both explanations.

"Mike, I have thought long and hard over our last conversation and I believe maybe I was a bit too precipitous, but that was where I was. There were ramifications particularly with my mother who had begun preparations for the wedding, and me too for that matter. I made the right decision at the time. However, after seeing your "Letters" (I was reluctant to read them but some kind of morbid curiosity got the best of me) at least I discovered you were not lying about the work in Brazil. My God, how that turned out! You got your new material on Chico's songs for "Letters" and then you, well, you went over the top with the music, Chico and the rest. I can only surmise you had some fun along with it, and I don't know the details; I guess it was 'same 'ole, same 'ole.' It appears to me you indeed are "done" with Brazil for a while. Is there anything you want to tell me?"

"Molly, you've got most of the story. The upshot is I'm back to college professor, will try to get back to some state of normalcy, but these good things keep happening. I mean the book signing tomorrow night. And more importantly at least getting a chance to talk to you. I can only assume by the fact you are here that there's some chance for at least a détente in our conflict, and maybe a breakthrough. Pardon my lousy political language; it's much more personal and important than that. I have still very deep feelings for you. Stuff happens and it happened to us. I like the idea of like you said "an exploration" and maybe a new beginning. I did return to "bachelor days" behavior in Rio, what else can you expect after the lowering the boom like you did? Once again, there was no pre-plan for anything amorous with Cristina Maria, just the help with Chico. You might get a kick out of one thing – I had a long confession with a Benedictine Monk! Ha! The rest as they say is "history."

"Okay for now," said Molly, "I'm happy to see you and ask myself why, but here I am. Water under the bridge, but a very shaky bridge. What do you have in store for me that won't rile me? Oh, and maybe I can satisfy your tardy interest in me at dinner."

"I want to take you to the Met Museum of Art this afternoon, have a nice dinner at the place of your choice, and want you to be my guest at the signing tomorrow. You are the one who has been to Greenwich Village and can maybe show me around before the signing, it's at 6 p.m. tomorrow. I'm very nervous it will be me, you, James Hansen and an empty room. I'd like for you to sit by me at the book table; that would be my honor."

"All this sounds good, I'll take you up on the tourism and dinner, but I'll be in the back of the room at the signing. Okay?"

We did the art museum, Molly my guide since she was the one who really knew Modern Art; but I was more excited about the Spanish Gallery. Dinner was a candle light affair with a bottle of champagne, and even some laughter recalling our former courtship and good times. There was a short explanation by Molly of her recent time and life in D.C., very short. She and Sherman were "back on" and she was not lonely. That's all. Molly said she still wasn't crazy about Sand Hill Cranes or tractors or corn or Big Red football, and wondered how I could be satisfied in

Lincoln. I laughed and said it seemed to be the only option. The next day would have its surprises.

James Hansen called me at the hotel, said all was ready for the book party, including refreshments handled by the "Times" and said he anticipated some New Yorkers interested in Brazil might be there. He would meet us at 5:30. I managed to say a thank you and see you then. Molly and I took the subway to the Village, she knowing her way around, and saying, "Wow, this has changed since my days." We entered the small book shop, were greeted by the owner, offered a glass of wine and the small talk, the book talk began. James sat at the table and introduced me, had many copies of the two books on hand, and offered an amazingly kind summary of my work, including background and how important Brazil was to the "Times." There were a couple dozen people from the public, many chattering away in Portuguese, ex-pats I figured. I spoke briefly of my love of Brazil, the research over the past years and added comments on the recent visit. Many folks had read the "Letters," fans by now I guessed; a few bought a book or two which I signed daring to add "Arretado, Mike Gaherty." There was one major surprise.

A well-dressed gentleman in coat and tie sidled up to me and introduced himself in Portuguese: "Mr. Gaherty, I'm Olegário Santos, and I am the cultural attaché of Brazil in New York. It is an immense pleasure to meet you and we Brazilians want you to know how much we appreciate your dedication and even more, your accounts of Brazil to the reading public. There is one small aside you might be interested in; I serve double duty here in New York. I am a minor figure also representing the DOPS here in your country, purely diplomatic of course, but a part of our surveillance of Brazilians who have chosen New York as a "respite" from life in Brazil. As you might figure, we read the "Letters" with rapt and close attention; incidentally we pass on our observations to Brazil and to some people you have met there. General Goeldi among them." He laughed. "We understand that this year's final 'Letter" is forthcoming and want to assure you it will get a careful reading. By the way, Heitor Dias says hello."

"I'm sure you will indeed. My final 'Letter' is in the works and I will be reporting on my last days in Rio and of course what precipitated my departure, the Merzog Affair. I assure you I will be honest and yet forthcoming. Thank you and send my regards to the General and a big 'abraço' to Heitor. We, as you probably know, have had many good times in Rio."

I forgot to say, in the middle of my own remarks to the people in the room, taking a deep breath, I said, "I'd like to introduce you to and acknowledge a big inspiration in my life, Molly. She is in the back row. Molly please accept the applause of our new friends here." She turned a bit red, but stood up and waved.

After the signing James Hansen said, "I'd like to take you to a nice restaurant we enjoy here, offer a toast to your work and talk a bit of the future. Is that all right?"

I stammered "Of course." James flagged down a taxi and took us, can you believe it to the Rainbow Room in Rockefeller Plaza. I felt like a guest of royalty, and Molly seemed to enjoy the moment as well. With all the chitchat, James' account of his job and some goings on at the International Section, he summed it all up with a renewed statement of our previous agreement to spend the next months with the final "Letter" and me putting together "Letters III" for publication. Once again he reiterated we should take it slowly, finish Brazil and in a year talk of any future plans, perhaps considering Colombia, Guatemala and Mexico. I thanked him, told him how this has all been a wonderful dream come true and promised work to be sent shortly to him. We bade our goodbyes, and Molly and I returned to the hotel, truly both of us exhausted by the events of that memorable day. We went to the hotel bar and reminisced and spoke only tentatively of the future. Hurry up and wait was the gist; we would talk by phone in a month or two with no promises on the part of either of us. I did indeed sleep on the Murphy Bed. Next morning after breakfast she caught the Amtrak to Washington D.C, with a hug and light kiss goodbye and I was back on a plane to Omaha and the great outback

36

TYING UP LOOSE ENDS IN LINCOLN

So, I settled in once again. Most of it was routine, preparing classes for Spring Term, sending he final "Letter" to James Hansen, mainly giving my take on the Merzog Affair, and a premonition of rough times for Brazil. One big distraction was the call from Sonia in Brazil wanting to know my news but mainly saying she could set up a reunion of sorts in San Francisco. My answer was, well, no. I explained I had met Molly in New York, that I had hopes for both of us to "see the light" and get back to old times. Sonia, a fit fiery as was her temperament did not take this well, saying I had broken a promise to meet her. That was not my recollection. At least she did not threaten me with any Rodrigues Limited reprisal, but said, "Miguel, I hope you and I don't regret this. I'm at the company now, my own corner office in Contracts, and I guess life goes on. I'm really sorry about all this; maybe someday you'll see what you missed. Right now, the offer is still on the table. I'll call again in a month or two and see if you have been "enlightened." I said, "No need for that Sonia. We had our good times, but like I said out at the Barra Beach, this life of yours is not for the farm boy, and there were no promises. Best of luck to you, but more for Brazil and the other Brazilians. I hope we can just be friends." The phone clicked and I sat wondering if I was an asshole for turning down that future.

Another surprise, more agreeable, was a wire payment to my bank with no less than a $2000 check from Philips Recording Company in Rio. Chico called the next day explaining that it was "Arretado's share" of concert proceeds. I thanked him, brought him up to date on events in New York, and Molly, and that the last "Letter" would tell the truth about recent events, i.e. Merzog. Chico encouraged me, saying it was the right thing to do. He closed with a laugh, saying that the invitation for Carnival in Rio was still pending, and also that he would be getting me out on the soccer field at his Politeama Private Stadium. "You've got some blanks to fill in on Brazil my friend." It was sad when we hung up, kind of a final chapter, at least for the near future. Chico promised to stay in touch with developments vis a vis the DOPS wiretapping his phone line. I wished him happiness with Marieta and the children and assured him I would be on the lookout for any new songs. Neither of us knew then the somber developments to come the following year.

Spring rolled around, it was good to be back in the classroom, after all, it was my first love and vocation. Classes went well and the Friday afternoon beer and pizza get together with wonderful Portuguese students of the Brazil club started up again. Regular calls, by that I mean once a month, came from Molly to me and vice versa, all friendly, all chatty but no new developments. Healing would take a long time. The good news is the calls kept coming.

That next year would bring good professional news. The book did indeed come out in Pernambuco with the title "A Literatura de Cordel" (suggested by Ariano Suassuna). Very Brazil-like, it came in the mail wrapped in that fragile mailing paper they use in Brazil, all torn on the outside. And a package came later with my twenty copies. Now I was set for an application for promotion which I did the same year. It along with the Casa de Rui "Studies" book plus articles in good academic journals in Brazil and the U.S. carried the day. "Letters from Brazil" was not considered "academic" by my colleagues but the majority of people on the committee recognized their significant publicity value for me, the department and the U. of Nebraska. I modestly add that no one else could speak of such a contribution from a professor in the "outback." With tenure and Associate Professor in my pocket it allowed for me to relax a bit, continue with research projects and classes, and most important, move on to "home security," i.e. more calls to Molly.

37

SILENCE

Later in 1971 a perhaps predictable end came to it all. The news was a new album by Chico and his musical partner Gilberto Gil and perhaps his best song – commentary on the current times in Brazil. "Cálice" ["Chalice"]. It goes a long way to explain how things were turning worse in Brazil, sad times indeed. The lyrics were roundly prohibited by the Censorship Board, but the song was released and sold like hotcakes anyway. The glitch was in a live performance in São Paulo. Chico and Gil decided to just hum the melody without lyrics, and punctuated each line with the word "Cálice." Phonogram (formerly Philips) cut the sound to the microphones. This, secondarily, ended Chico's relationship with them and brought a contract with a new company. I'm reporting the song here, limited by copyright, but with the usual prose explanation after.

"Cálice" [Chalice] was ostensibly the story of Jesus's passion when He asked his father to take the ensuing events away from him:
"Pai, afasta de mim esse cálice de vinho tinto de sangue …
"Father, take this chalice of red wine with the tint of blood from me …
"Como beber dessa bebida amarga, tragar a dor, engulir a labuta …
"How can I drink this bitter drink, swallow the pain, devour the labor …
"De que me vale ser filho da santa, melhor ser filho da outra …
"What is it worth to me being the son of the saint, better of another…

Filling in some of the lines of the rest of the song, in my own partial paraphrasing: Even with a closed mouth, one's heart remains. I would hope for

135

another reality, less morbid, with fewer lies, with less brute force. How difficult it is to wake up silenced in the silence of the night. It's this silence that kills me. What good it is to have good will when only the silence is left. I'd like to invent my own sin, to die of my own poison, drink myself to death until they forget me.

"Father, take this chalice from me."

The song thus in its most apparent reading is the lamentation of Christ before his coming passion. But <u>between the lines</u> is the alternative message: the Portuguese word "Cálice" can be taken phonetically to be "Cale-se" or "Be silent!" For the majority of the knowing Brazilians it is no less than the Regime's dictum for Chico, and, extrapolated, for other composers and singers, for the press, for the politicians, for all Brazilians opposed to the Dictatorship. It was the last straw, the straw that broke the camel's back.

"Cálice" - "Be silent"

Silence.

EPILOGUE

Mike Gaherty did not return to Brazil for seven years until better times.

ABOUT THE AUTHOR

Mark Curran is a retired professor from Arizona State University where he worked from 1968 to 2011. He taught Spanish and Portuguese and their respective cultures. His research specialty was Brazil and its "popular poetry in verse" or the "literatura de cordel," and he has published many articles in research reviews and now some sixteen books related to the "cordel" in Brazil, the United States and Spain. Other books done during retirement are of either an autobiographic nature – "The Farm" or "Coming of Age with the Jesuits" - or reflect classes taught at ASU on Luso-Brazilian Civilization, Latin American Civilization or Spanish taught at ASU. The latter are in the series "Stories I Told My Students:" books on Brazil, Colombia, Guatemala, Mexico, Portugal and Spain. "Letters from Brazil" is an early experiment combining reporting and fiction, and "A Professor Takes to the Sea" is a chronicle of a retirement adventure with Lindblad Expeditions - National Geographic Explorer. "Letters from Brazil II" is a continued experiment in combining facts and fiction, but more fiction. "Rural Odyssey – Living Can Be Dangerous" is more of the same. And now "Letters from Brazil III" continues the Mike Gaherty chronicle.

Published Books

A Literatura de Cordel. Brasil. 1973
Jorge Amado e a Literatura de Cordel. Brasil. 1981
A Presença de Rodolfo Coelho Cavalcante na Moderna Literatura de Cordel. Brasil. 1987
La Literatura de Cordel – Antología Bilingüe – Español y Portugués. España. 1990
Cuíca de Santo Amaro Poeta-Repórter da Bahia. Brasil. 1991
História do Brasil em Cordel. Brasil. 1998

Cuíca de Santo Amaro – Controvérsia no Cordel. Brasil. 2000

Brazil's Folk-Popular Poetry – "a Literatura de Cordel" – a Bilingual Anthology in English and Portuguese. USA. 2010

The Farm – Growing Up in Abilene, Kansas, in the 1940s and the 1950s. USA. 2010

Retrato do Brasil em Cordel. Brasil. 2011

Coming of Age with the Jesuits. USA. 2012

Peripécias de um Pesquisador "Gringo" no Brasil nos Anos 1960 ou 'A Cata de Cordel" USA. 2012

Adventures of a 'Gringo' Researcher in Brazil in the 1960s or In Search of Cordel. USA. 2012

A Trip to Colombia – Highlights of Its Spanish Colonial Heritage. USA. 2013

Travel, Research and Teaching in Guatemala and Mexico – In Quest of the Pre-Columbian Heritage

> Volume I – Guatemala. 2013
> Volume II – Mexico. USA. 2013

A Portrait of Brazil in the Twentieth Century – The Universe of the "Literatura de Cordel." USA. 2013

Fifty Years of Research on Brazil – A Photographic Journey. USA. 2013

Relembrando - A Velha Literatura de Cordel e a Voz dos Poetas. USA. 2014

Aconteceu no Brasil – Crônicas de um Pesquisador Norte Americano no Brasil II, USA. 2015

It Happened in Brazil – Chronicles of a North American Researcher in Brazil II. USA, 2015

Diário de um Pesquisador Norte-Americano no Brasil III. USA, 2016

Diary of a North American Researcher in Brazil III. USA, 2016

Letters from Brazil. A Cultural-Historical Narrative Made Fiction. USA 2017.

A Professor Takes to the Sea – Learning the Ropes on the National Geographic Explorer.

> Volume I, "Epic South America" 2013 USA, 2018.
> Volume II, 2014 and "Atlantic Odyssey 108" 2018

Letters from Brazil II – Research, Romance and Dark Days Ahead. USA, 2019.

A Rural Odyssey – Living Can Be Dangerous. USA, 2019.
Letters from Brazil III – Good Times to Sad Times. USA. 2020.

Professor Curran lives in Mesa, Arizona, and spends part of the year in Colorado. He is married to Keah Runshang Curran and they have one daughter Kathleen who lives in Albuquerque, New Mexico, married to teacher Courtney Hinman in 2018. Her documentary film "Greening the Revolution" was presented most recently in the Sonoma Film Festival in California, this after other festivals in Milan, Italy and New York City. Katie was named best female director in the Oaxaca Film Festival in Mexico.

The author's e-mail address is: profmark@asu.edu

His website address is: www.currancordelconnection.com

Printed in the United States
By Bookmasters